Conjure Island

Also by Eden Royce
Root Magic

Conjure Island

EDEN ROYCE

WALDEN POND PRESS

An Imprint of HarperCollinsPublishers

Library of Congress Control Number: 2020947638
ISBN 978-0-06-289961-3

Typography by Joel Tippie
22 23 24 25 26 LBC 6 5 4 3 2

First Edition

For the lost.
I hope you find your portal.

New brooms sweep clean, but old ones get the corners.
—Gullah Geechee proverb

The South is a portal.
—Sara Makeba Daise

1

Del Baker was lost.

Not lost in the way you might think; she knew where she was—next to her gramma in the passenger seat of their truck as they left Interstate 95 and merged onto Route 1. They were moving. Again. This time from Hanscom Air Force Base in Massachusetts to Dover Air Force Base in Delaware. Leaving behind everything Del had known for the past year.

No, Del was lost in another way. She felt disconnected from everything around her, like she was drifting in an ocean without any land in sight. Each year when her dad changed duty stations and she and Gramma had to pack

1

up their lives and move, Del couldn't help but think about the one piece of their family that wasn't moving with them. The piece that had never come with them.

Her mom.

Dad and Gramma never talked about Mom. When Del used to ask about her, Dad would have some assessment to complete or a work meeting he'd forgotten about and he would stride away. Her gramma would redirect, usually reminding Del she had chores or homework or that she needed to check the garage for anything they might have overlooked when packing.

Del was a kid, but she wasn't stupid. She knew what they were doing. She just couldn't figure out how to make her dad and gramma tell her anything about her mom. Del's mom had died while giving birth to her and she knew it was probably hard for them to talk about her. But it was even harder for Del, not knowing anything about her.

What was her favorite movie? What kind of ice cream did she like? Did she read a lot like Del? If so, what was the book she read over and over until she knew the words by heart? Anything so she could feel connected to her mother. Their whole family was so small—just her, Gramma, and Dad—so she wanted to include memories of her mom as a part of it. But she didn't have any and neither her gramma nor her dad wanted to share theirs. And so, even if Del didn't stop thinking about Mom, she stopped asking. She set her questions aside, just like she'd set aside her memories of each town they'd lived in, each year they moved. Del would shed them, like a snake does its old skin.

She didn't want to remember. Remembering hurt. Besides, what was the point? She wasn't going to return to any of the places. They never did. It was best that she leave those memories in the past and focus on starting over. Again.

Del tucked one of her long braids behind her ear and looked out the window at the gray asphalt of the highway, rocking slightly as the cars in the fast lane whizzed by. There was no use feeling bad for herself. Moving, thinking about Mom . . . these things were hard on Dad and Gramma as well. And it was all of their jobs to take care of one another. That thought, at least, made Del smile.

"Get ready to throw the money," Del's grandmother said, breaking Del out of her thoughts. She pulled their truck in behind the line of cars on the Delaware Turnpike.

"Already on it," Del said, pulling two handfuls of coins from the front zippered pocket of her backpack. She was the one who'd told Gramma they needed real money for the tollbooth, not credit or debit cards. She'd looked it all up online and read the information given in her dad's transfer packet.

The weight of the coins was heavy and she shifted them all to one hand while she wiped the other palm on her jeans. She despised moving. Moving meant a new town, a new school, learning where the grocery stores and pharmacies were, and what kind of shows came on regular TV. At least this move was at the beginning of the summer, which was definitely better than the one that happened two cities ago, the week before school started. That year had been awful.

"Nervous?" Gramma asked, inching the car up in the line.

Del shrugged and jangled the coins. "Eh, you know."

"No, I don't know. That's why I asked," Gramma said. "It's a lot, moving again."

"Nope, I'm okay," Del said, flicking through her phone.

What was the point of saying she didn't want to move again? They were already on the road. In fact, they were almost there. Right now, the only thing she was nervous about was their stuff arriving at their new house on time and undamaged. Once, the movers had broken their TV and it had taken forever for it to get replaced.

The car radio crackled, losing the station. Del pushed the button until a new station came in clear, without fuzzy static. When music started drifting through the speakers, she sat back. It was a station that played music from the sixties, seventies, and eighties. Del and Gramma both loved oldies.

Even though moves were easier when Dad was with them and not out on deployment, Del looked forward to the road trips with just her and Gramma. They danced in their seats when their favorite songs came on, pointed out landmarks and the weird things people did in their cars on the highway. Once Del had seen a man driving with his foot hanging out the window. She wondered what he would do if his shoe fell off in the middle of the interstate. The idea of him pulling his car over to look for it made her laugh. Gramma laughed too when Del told her.

Still, this move had been more rushed than usual. When Dad was transferred, they'd had to work overtime to get everything in order. Several nights, Gramma had let her stay up late to make sure they were all packed up. While Del hated moving, Gramma was stressed. She'd also been moving a little slower, but when Del asked her about it, she smiled and said it was because she was tired from packing and from answering questions from nosy granddaughters. Once they were in the new house, they could both relax.

Gramma took a few different medicines for her blood pressure, and Del made sure the pill bottles were packed in a bag that went in the car with them and not accidentally dumped into the boxes to be loaded on the big moving truck. Del kept up with her grandmother's medicines by setting reminders on her phone, and Gramma always said she was grateful for the help. She also promised to get some rest when they got settled. And once Dad was home, they could all be a family together again. They were planning to surprise him when he was back from maneuvers or whatever, by having their new home already decorated and looking good.

"I worry about you, you know." Gramma looked in the rearview mirror, then down at Del beside her. "You're only eleven. That's young to have this much responsibility."

Del shook her head. "It's okay. I don't mind. And I can definitely handle it."

"I know. I suppose I'm hoping we'll have two or three years in one place this time. Give you the chance to make some friends, do whatever it is kids do nowadays."

"I don't need friends," Del said. "I have you."

Gramma made a sound in the back of her throat. "I'm talking about kids your own age."

Del didn't want to argue. She pocketed her phone and looked out the passenger-side window at the rest of the cars lining up to get through the toll plaza. That's when the radio crackled again for a moment, then the DJ's voice came through clear as melting ice.

"Here's a classic for you old heads, a throwback to the days of bell-bottom jeans and disco queens. This quiet storm love ballad is 'Not Another Day' by one-hit wonder Violet Vesey."

Del smiled as she listened to the familiar song: the soft *ta-ta-tap* of drum brooms, the dancing flute, the mellow piano intro she'd heard so many times but still loved. She swayed side to side in her seat, eyes closed while the song washed over her like waves as she sang along:

6

There's an empty space
that used to be his place
Here within my heart

Heartache should have brought us close
Now when I need you the most
You have disappeared

There's a wall between us
Even in the hall I can't see us
Ever getting to okay.

Gramma shifted uncomfortably in embarrassment. But Del smiled and nudged her, and just sang along even louder.

I stand under my oak tree
And wonder why you can't see
That I'm barely holding on

And so I'm leaving
On that bus this evening
Why can't you ask me to stay?

But as the song was about to get to the chorus, her grandmother reached over and turned the radio off.

Del's eyes sprang open. "Gramma! That's your song!

The one you're famous for!"

"And you've heard it many times before. We're talking about you finding yourself a life."

"I love that song. Just because it's about your ex-boyfriend or whatever doesn't mean I'm too young to get it." Del pouted, pulling her phone back out from her jeans pocket. "I can understand things, even if I haven't experienced them myself."

"Is that right?" Gramma asked, her eyebrow arched.

"Yep. And I don't need friends my age."

Gramma sighed and turned the radio back on, but kept the volume low so it didn't interrupt their conversation. "You are an amazing kid, baby. I know it's hard not having deep roots, lots of family ties. You should at least try to make some friends."

They were at the tollbooth window now. Del unbuckled her seat belt and leaned over her grandmother. The scent of Gramma's cocoa butter lotion was warm and sweet on her skin, and Del inhaled it before throwing the handful of coins into the big mesh net attached to the booth. She sat down and buckled herself back in while the coins clattered and spun, wiggling and shifting the net as they finally clunked down. The screen flashed from red to green. The tollbooth attendant gave them a thumbs-up and the barrier arm preventing them from moving forward lifted. They waved as Gramma stepped on the gas.

They motored down the road for a while, the only

sound in the car Gramma's voice drifting through the speakers, singing a song from long before Del was born. Del sang along with the chorus under her breath.

Ask me back to stay
Cause I can't take
Not another day living this way
Without you

It had been a long time since Gramma joined in. These days, when Del put one of her songs on, she most often sat there until it was over. Even now, Gramma was concentrating on driving, her expression blank. Maybe the song hurt to hear and Gramma didn't want to discuss it. At least she'd turned the radio back on, maybe that was some kind of progress.

Once the song was over, Del spoke. "I used to try and make friends," she admitted. "But I don't bother anymore. I'm always the new kid until the year is almost over. Then it's time to leave for the next place where I'll be the new one again. Kids always promise to keep in touch, but they never do."

"Oh, honey . . ."

Del didn't like the sound in her grandmother's voice. She didn't want anyone feeling bad for her. She was fine. Sure, sometimes Del wondered what it would be like to have a big family, like some of the other kids she'd met.

And she wondered what it was like to live in one place your whole entire life. But it wasn't her job to wish things were different. It was her job to help hold things together when Dad wasn't around.

"It's okay." Del smoothed her long braids out of her face and secured them at the back of her neck with a satin scrunchie. "We'll do what we always do: finish the move and be there for each other until Dad tells us it's time to move again."

"Hmm" was all Gramma said. She looked in her mirrors, changed lanes. "I think the exit is coming up here soon."

Del pulled up the directions on her phone. "It's in four more miles on the right."

"Thank you, baby."

A beep sounded on Del's phone. "The movers are already at our new house. How'd they get there before us?"

Gramma glanced sideways at Del. "Maybe because they didn't feel like the world would stop turning if they didn't get a turkey burger and a cream soda at Frosty's Diner."

Del poked her bottom lip out. "But it was Frosty's! You know they're my favorite. I didn't even know there was a Frosty's on the way here. We had to stop." She did a little wiggle dance in her seat. "And the sweet potato fries were so good!"

"They were good—hot and crispy. Just the way I like them." Gramma smiled.

"Me too!"

Gramma took the exit Del indicated toward their new home.

When they finally arrived and Gramma announced "here we are!" her voice was full of exhaustion. Driving wasn't her favorite thing to do, and it was one of the few things Del couldn't do to help out. Not yet. In most states, she'd have to be fifteen before she could get her learner's permit, which would allow her to drive when Gramma or Dad was in the car with her. Four more years.

Gramma pulled the car in close to the garage door of their new house. They always lived off base and would typically find someplace cheap so they could keep any extra money from Dad's housing allowance in a college fund for Del. The Make-UR-Move truck was parked by the curb in front of the house and three men were waiting by it. Del climbed out, pulling on her backpack and keeping her phone at the ready. Gramma got out with a groan and jangled the keys as they walked to the front door. She dropped them once before she could get them in the lock.

"We can have them bring the couch in first. Then you can sit down. I got this." Del took her sunglasses off her face and sat them on top of her head, wiggling the arms of the frames to get them between her braids.

"I'm fine." Gramma shifted her handbag higher on her

shoulder and leaned into a stretch with her palms pressed to her lower back.

It was Del's turn to regard her grandmother sternly. "You're tired."

"What about the movers? Who's gonna tell them where to put things?"

"You know I can show them where everything goes."

Gramma pushed the door open and they headed inside. "Okay, young lady."

After Del instructed the movers where the sofas, beds, chairs, and tables should be placed, they didn't need much more help. All the boxes were labeled with the name of the room they belonged in, so Del joined Gramma in the kitchen to watch. Within an hour and a half, it was finished. The movers had Gramma sign a form and they gave her one copy of it. Del gave each of the movers a cool bottle of water and wished them well as they drove away.

"Home sweet home," Gramma said, looking around the new house with her hands on her hips.

"I guess," Del replied, taking off her sunglasses and placing them on the kitchen counter. "We'd better get started on making it that way."

2

Del inspected all the boxes until she found the one she'd marked with a red *F* in felt-tip pen. This was the box they always opened first, because it had everything they needed immediately upon arriving at the new house. Some silverware, a few cups and plates, napkins, salt and pepper, a few other spices and herbs. Bathroom tissue, two pump bottles of hand soap. A little wireless speaker, her grandmother's homemade cleaner that smelled like lemongrass mixed with pine, some cleaning rags, and a dustpan. She placed the items on their bare kitchen table.

"Something's missing . . . ," Gramma said, tapping her bottom lip with her finger.

"Oh!" Del grabbed the keys from the counter and went to the car. From the back seat she grabbed the broom, mop, and bucket and brought them inside.

"I knew you wouldn't forget." Gramma was waiting for Del to return. She'd already combined salt with dried rose petals and sprinkled the mixture in every corner of the house.

"Of course not," Del said. "We've got to clean out any bad stuff from this new place so we can have a fresh start." She turned on the speaker, connected her phone to it, and found a stream of the radio station that had played Gramma's song earlier.

"Start at the back of the house and sweep toward the front. Then we'll dump all that dust and dirty water out." Gramma placed the mop head on the floor and held the handle like a microphone. "Ready?"

Del did the same with the broom handle. "Ready."

Singing along to every oldie that came on, dancing and swaying to the beat, they cleaned the entire house. Del swept up the salt and rose petals, and Gramma finished by mopping with the scented cleaning wash. They swept and scrubbed the whole place until it smelled fresh and clean and every surface sparkled. Lemony pine scent floated on the air, making the house that had sat empty for months feel renewed.

When they were finished, Gramma wrung out the mop and stored it. Then she carefully cleaned all the dust and dirt from the bristles of the broom and stood it in a corner next to the refrigerator. Del dropped the dustpan next to it.

"Whew!" Gramma said, falling into a chair at the kitchen table. "I am worn out."

"We haven't even unpacked anything yet," Del said, checking the list on her phone. "We usually put towels and stuff in the bathroom and get sheets on the beds before we stop for a break."

Gramma fanned herself with her hands. "I know, baby, but I'm gonna have to take a rest earlier than that today. My head is swinging. Better take my pills."

Del glanced at the clock on her phone. They'd been so busy working, she'd almost forgotten it was time for Gramma's medicine. She grabbed one of the glasses she'd unpacked and filled it with water from the tap. She brought it over, along with Gramma's handbag.

With trembling hands, Gramma fished a plastic pillbox from her bag and popped open the lid on the section marked *S* for Saturday. She dumped a white and a blue tablet into her palm and swallowed them with water.

"You're going to have to eat something in about thirty minutes," Del said. "We only have some crackers and honey-roasted peanuts left in the bag from the car."

Gramma closed her eyes and nodded.

"I can go to the grocery store," Del said. "Maybe get what we need to make some spaghetti and a salad." She opened the maps app on her phone to find the nearest store. Surely, there was one close enough to walk to.

Her gramma chuckled. "No, no. Just . . . use that device of yours to order us something. We never make extra work on our first night, right? Is there a pizza place around here?"

"Oooh, pizza! I'll check." Del tapped on her phone.

"I'll rest my eyes while you do." She leaned her head against the wall of the kitchen and closed her eyes.

There were three pizzerias that delivered to their new address; Del picked the closest one. She liked the look of the mascot: a giant pizza wearing high-top sneakers. She ordered a small chicken sausage pizza for herself and a pasta dish with peas and asparagus that she knew Gramma would like. While she waited for the food, Del found the towels and put them in the bathroom, along with the tissues and one of the soap dispensers. She also found sheets for the beds, but it was harder to make the bed on her own; she could get one side of the fitted sheet on, but when she went around to tug the other side, the elastic from the first side popped off. It was almost like someone invisible was messing with her.

"Ugh!" Del groaned.

She grabbed one of her boxes of books and sat it on the corner of the sheet she'd just put on, weighing it down. Then she went over to the other side and tugged at the loose end of the sheet, pulling it tight. The heavy books held the first side on so she could get the second one in place. After that, she finished the task in record time.

"Done." She removed the box and brushed her hands off on her jeans. Gramma would be pleased to see she had finished both beds so she could lie down if she wanted to.

Del finally took the time to give the house a real once-over. It was larger than the last place they'd lived, and it had a basement. Otherwise, it looked a lot like many of the houses they'd lived in. The towns and cities they'd spent time in were each a little different, but they all sort of blended together in her mind. No place stood out as the one she loved most or hated most. They'd probably be here for a year or so, and she could deal with almost any living situation for that long. Especially if the pizza was good.

At that moment, the doorbell rang.

Del raced downstairs to find Gramma already at the front door, holding two brown cardboard boxes stacked on top of each other, as well as a bag with two bottles of water.

"Thank you," she said to the delivery driver with a smile. She kept that smile for Del when she held up the boxes and asked, "Ready for dinner?"

"Yes!" Del pumped her fist in the air. "I made our beds, Gramma."

She lowered the boxes so Del could take the top one and they both headed to the kitchen. "Thank you, baby."

Del and Gramma mostly cooked meals from scratch at

home, so they could both be sure to keep healthy—something even more important for Gramma these days. But having a meal delivered on their first night in a new place was their tradition and a nice break from doing dishes and cleaning the kitchen.

Del went over to the big table in the dining room, but Gramma gestured toward the kitchen. "I'm not sure I can eat in there," she said once they sat down. "Who puts white carpet in a dining room?"

Del shrugged. "Maybe the people who lived here before weren't clumsy," she said. "Can you imagine trying to clean Kool-Aid out of it? I'd be too scared to drop something in there."

"So would I." Then she leaned closer to Del and said in a loud whisper, "Let's not go in there unless we have to. There's plenty of other rooms we can be comfortable in."

"Deal," Del said with a grin and bit into a slice. So good. Hanging out with her gramma and not having to do dishes? Even better.

Gramma twisted her pasta around her fork. She always used the forks they'd packed in their marked box because she hated using the plastic ones that came with delivery meals. So there would be a fork and a glass to wash later. Del could do that easy.

As they ate, Del looked around at the rest of the house that she could see from her chair. There was a door to a basement room on the underground level. On the first floor where they now sat, the kitchen looked into the massive living room on the right, and the white dining room on the left. A small bathroom and an office were off the living room. Upstairs, there were three bedrooms and a full-size bathroom.

"Can we paint this time?" So often they didn't take the time to paint the walls. They would have to paint back over it before they moved, and Dad never thought it was worth the extra trouble.

"Hm . . . we'll see what your father says when he gets here." Gramma sipped her water and blew out a long breath.

"You okay?" Del was instantly worried. "There's a pharmacy two blocks away in case we need to get anything."

"You're a smart girl, Del. I appreciate your research and all, but I'm fine." Gramma put down her fork. "I'll finish this pasta tomorrow. Way more than one meal here."

Del nodded. She'd munched through half her pizza, but it was too much to eat at one time. She closed the cardboard box, stacked her Gran's smaller one on top, and put them in the fridge.

"You can rest there while I unpack some boxes."

"Okay, baby. You go ahead." Gramma let out a heavy sigh and closed her eyes. "I'll help you in a while."

Del got to work unpacking, starting with the plates and pots and pans. She placed these in cabinets in the kitchen, then moved on to a box labeled "Living Room." Inside was a bunch of different vases covered in bubble wrap that Dad had sent Gramma from different countries he'd visited. Carefully, she unwrapped them and set them around the room: two on the mantelpiece of the fireplace, one on the small table in the hallway, and three grouped together on the big coffee table in the center of the room.

There was only one box out of place, a box labeled "Gramma" that should have gone upstairs to her room. She'd carry it up and Gramma could unpack it when she felt better. Del tried to lift the box, but it was *heavy*. One of her braids slipped out of her scrunchie and she flipped it out of her face. Again she tried to lift the box, but she couldn't.

She glanced over to the kitchen, but Gramma still had her eyes closed and her head back against the wall, making a soft snoring sound. "That's okay," she whispered. "I'll unpack the box until it's light enough to carry myself."

She pulled the wide strip of tape away and opened the box. Del had never unpacked for Gramma before; they always let each other take care of their own rooms, so Del had no idea what could be so heavy. Inside were the items Gramma always had in her room: a mirrored tray she kept her perfumes on, also bundled in bubble wrap, a small folding fan, and a gold-colored jewelry box with legs and feet like a lion. Del set these aside to place on the dresser in Gramma's room later.

It was what was under these things that caught Del's attention. Something she'd never seen before.

Nestled under one of Gramma's homemade quilts was a small blue leather case. Del removed it from the box and sat it on her lap. It felt heavy for its size and looked a lot like the black briefcase her dad took to work, only smaller. Dad's briefcase had his initials on it, but there was nothing on the tag attached to the handle of this case.

Without thinking, Del moved her fingers to the shiny brass buttons on either side of the handle. Each button had a lock on it, so maybe the case wouldn't even open. But when Del pressed the left and right buttons at the same time, the case let out a soft click and the clasps holding the lid closed flipped up. She held her breath as she lifted the lid and peered inside.

Inside lay a newspaper with an old picture of Del's grandmother on the front page, the edges turning brittle and brown. Also inside was a round silver ball on a short, curved handle and several other items she didn't recognize. Del reached to pull them out, but her grandmother's shadow fell over her at that moment, stopping her in her tracks.

"Are those yours?" she asked in a sharper tone than Del was used to.

Del jumped. She hadn't heard Gramma move out of her seat. "No, ma'am. But I thought . . ." She pulled out the silver thing. "What is this?"

21

"You just get into everything, don't you?" She took the item from Del's fingers. "It's a baby's rattle."

"Was it mine?"

Gramma shook her head. "It was mine when I was a baby, and then your mother's when she was a baby."

Del tried to get a better look at the rattle, but Gramma quickly snatched the case from Del's lap and replaced the item inside.

Gramma would often talk about when she was a young up-and-coming singer, but Del couldn't remember the last time Gramma had talked about when she was a kid. Just like she did when Del asked for stories about her mom, Gramma would change the subject anytime Del asked where she'd grown up and what she was like at Del's age, saying it wasn't anything interesting. But the things in that box *did* look interesting. They looked like stories, and Del was hungry for stories about her mom and gramma.

"How come I've never seen it before?" she asked.

"I . . . put this one away after your mother died."

Del's breath caught in her in her throat. "Why?"

Gramma closed the case and rested both her hands on top of it. "I'd rather not talk about it, honey."

"Okay." Like the lyrics of her gramma's song talking about lost romance, Del didn't need to experience something in order to understand it. She also didn't want to upset Gramma when she wasn't feeling well.

Del kept her questions about her mom buried deep

down in her own sort of box. She supposed it was all right that Gramma did too.

"I know you have questions about your mother," Gramma went on. "Maybe even about my family, where you came from, but . . . ." She swallowed hard, like she was using all her effort to hold herself together. Her hands shook.

Del and her gramma didn't have anyone else to rely on when Dad was away, but they'd never needed anyone else. Del knew some kids had big families where there were lots of brothers and sisters and cousins and aunts and uncles, but she couldn't imagine what that was even like.

It had always been the three of them. There was no one to visit for special events like weddings or graduations and no one came to their house for celebrations. They didn't cook big meals for holidays like families on TV. Even though a part of Del wanted to have roots and connections to larger family, she'd never admit it because Gramma worked so hard to keep their tiny family together. Adding to her problems was the last thing she wanted to do.

So Del smiled, even though she didn't really feel like it. This was their life: the moving, the new schools, the starting over each and every year. Nothing would change that.

"It's okay. You don't have to talk about it." She leaned her head on Gramma's arm and breathed in her soft, cocoa-butter scent. "It's not that I don't wish my mom was still alive. But you and Dad are all the family I need."

Gramma's arm wrapped around Del. "I did all I could raising you."

"I know," she said. "And look how great I turned out."

The sound of Gramma's laughter was all Del wanted to hear and she snuggled closer. "So you think you're all grown-up now?" she said after they stopped laughing.

"Almost," Del confirmed. Seeing her grandmother's look of worry, she added, "I'm all right."

"You sure, baby?"

Del hugged her tight, and when Gramma hugged her back, rocking her to and fro, Del knew she was in the best place in the world.

3

A strange noise woke Del in the middle of the night.

She blinked, confused for a moment as to where she was. A second later, she remembered. She was in her old bed but in a new room, in a new city.

It had been hard to fall sleep. She was used to noise at night—cars on the street, people talking as they walked by, dogs barking—and the quiet here was disturbing. How could you sleep when the night was so silent? It felt as if there was nothing beyond the walls of this house, just empty space. The thought made her anxious.

But she must have eventually fallen asleep, because she was wide awake now. Her bedside clock showed it was past midnight. She rubbed her face, careful not to disturb the satin scarf she tied her braids back with to sleep.

The sound that woke her came again. It was a scraping sound, coming from downstairs. Del was instantly alert. The house had been vacant for a while before they moved in; maybe someone thought it still was and was trying to break in. She slid out of bed and shoved her feet into her sneakers without socks. The shorts and T-shirt she slept in would allow her to run, to get Gramma, to fight if she had to. Should she get a weapon? Something to scare off a burglar . . . but what? She glanced around her room. She hadn't finished unpacking, but even if she had, she didn't have anything to scare intruders—no baseball bat or golf club or anything.

She did, however, have a really heavy trophy she'd won for reading the most books over a summer last year. She grabbed it. While she was happy she'd won, it didn't help her make any friends at her new school. All the local kids thought she'd lied about the number of books she'd read. But it wasn't her fault that she spent all her summers reading books. She loved to get lost in the crisp pages that described new worlds to her. Living inside those books made her feel less lost in her own world. The friends she made in books, she could visit anytime she wanted.

The sound came again, breaking apart Del's thoughts. It was like someone was rummaging through a box downstairs. Had someone watched them move in and decided to rob them on their first night in this house? She *knew* they should have had an alarm system installed.

She slipped out her room and tiptoed down the hall, careful not to disturb Gramma as she snuck by her room. The door was closed. Good. She could handle this. Del transferred the trophy from one hand to the other while she wiped her palms on her shorts to get a better grip.

Del padded down the staircase, the trophy held high. At the bottom, she paused. Waited for the sound to come again. There it was. She followed it around the corner to the living room where they'd left several boxes destined for the small bathroom or the coat closet in the hallway. She didn't realize how many boxes hadn't been put away. She really should have—

The rummaging sound stopped suddenly, only to be replaced by a shriek of pain unlike anything Del had ever heard before. Somewhere in that cry, she recognized the voice.

"Gramma!"

Del dropped the trophy and ran toward the sound. She found her grandmother in the hallway between the small bathroom and the office, bent over and clutching the wall for support. Several of the boxes had been cut or torn open, and sticky brown tape clung to her gramma's hands and her robe.

Del went to help her but backed away when her gramma held up her hand.

"What's wrong, Gramma? What's going on?"

Her grandmother eyes were squinched closed, like she was trying to trap her pain behind them. But it was no use, her breath hissed out like air escaping a balloon. "My leg. Like . . . electricity . . . shooting through it." Gramma's breath was coming faster and faster even though she was barely moving. She gritted out her next words from behind clenched teeth. "Burning. Buzzing. My whole left side is buzzing something fierce."

Del didn't know what to do. She'd never seen her gramma like this. She'd never seen anyone like this. She wanted to know what the pain Gramma was describing meant, but her phone was upstairs in her room and she didn't want to leave Gramma even for a second to go get it.

"Sit down." It was the first thing that came to her mind. Gramma usually felt better after she sat a while.

"Can't. Can't move."

With a high-pitched cry, Gramma did finally move. But it wasn't to sit down. Her legs started to give way and she sank toward the floor. Del ran to her and held her around the waist, trying to keep her up or move her to the sofa, she couldn't decide which. But it was impossible. Gramma was too heavy. She couldn't stay upright, so her entire body weight pressed in on Del's arms and shoulders. With every bit of strength she had, Del tried to keep her gramma from falling—

Both Del and Gramma collapsed to the floor in the hallway. Del landed first, and it was all she could do to keep Gramma's head from hitting the floor. She didn't know much first aid, but she knew not to let someone's head crack on a hard surface. Del leaned close; Gramma's eyes were closed, and her breathing was still coming hard and fast. Way too fast. That wasn't good. Gramma's moans of pain were so horrible Del felt sick.

Why couldn't Dad just be here for once? Why wasn't anyone here to help?

No, she couldn't think like that. Del was the one who was here, so she was the one who had to do something.

"It's gonna be okay, Gramma. I'll be right back."

Del raced upstairs, grabbed her phone from the bedside table. She dialed 9-1-1 as she ran back. Sweat had formed on her gramma's face and neck, and her breathing was like she'd run a marathon. She was clutching at her side and the top of her leg. The light in the hallway was flickering, and as the phone rang, Del wanted to make a note to pack replacement light bulbs in their essentials box for their next move. Why was she thinking of stupid light bulbs?

When the operator picked up, Del clicked into gear. She gave the woman her name, and told her that her grandmother had collapsed after feeling pain like she was being electrocuted on one side of her body. The operator told her stay on the phone. Then she asked Del a bunch of questions, starting with their address. Thankfully, Del had it programmed into her phone. She was able to answer the other questions like how old her gramma was and what medications she took. The entire time, she held her gramma's hand.

"And how old are you?" the emergency operator asked.

"Eleven."

"Is there anyone else in the house? An adult?"

"Only me and Gramma," she said. "My dad is deployed."

The operator then asked for Dad's name and rank. "You're doing great, Del. An ambulance is on its way. Just hold on for a few more minutes, okay?"

Even though her heart felt like it was flapping around like a trapped bird, even though her stomach was twisted and sour with fear of losing one of the only two people she loved in the world, Del was holding on. She hoped Gramma was too. She pressed her hand to Gramma's heart and said, "I will."

Del had been sitting in the hospital's waiting area for what felt like hours awaiting news about her grandmother's condition. Every so often, a nurse would check on her, asking her if she needed anything. She shook her head, hoping someone could tell her what was going on soon.

Finally, a man dressed in pale green scrubs came into the waiting room. When he spotted Del, he made a bee-line directly to her.

"Are you Del Baker?" When she nodded, he said, "I'm Jesse."

"Is my gramma okay?"

"She was in a lot of pain, but we've given her something to help with that. She's a bit woozy, but awake. The doctor spoke with your father, and you can come with me to see her, if you'd like."

Del stood, and pulled her backpack over her shoulder. Then she followed Nurse Jesse down the hall to a recovery room.

Once inside, she ran to the bed where her grandmother lay. "Gramma!"

"Hey, easy," Nurse Jesse said. "Don't get her too worked up. Quiet voices."

Del nodded and drew closer to the bed. Gramma was propped up on a couple of large pillows; she looked tiny among them. She had wires attached to her arm and chest, and a breathing tube thing under her nose. Her hair was a mess and the hospital gown she wore was faded and frayed around the neck. But she was awake and that was what mattered.

There was a plastic pitcher of water on the bedside table, along with an old-school landline phone. A movable tray with a clear bowl of water on it was placed over the bed and Del moved it out of the way so she could get closer.

"Gramma," she whispered, her voice unsteady. "Are you okay?"

Her gramma reached out a trembling hand. Del held it. Then Gramma said something Del couldn't hear.

She leaned closer. "What did you say?"

"Shoulda told you, baby." A small, strange smile spread across her face, but she didn't exactly look exactly happy.

"Told me what?"

But Gramma shook her head and tried to sit up. Nurse Jesse hurried over and encouraged her to lie back down. Del squeezed her gramma's hand gently. It felt so thin and delicate, the skin fragile and dry.

"Water," Gramma mumbled. "Use the water."

"You want water?" Del reached for the pitcher on the table but her gramma brushed her hand away. "What's going on with her? Is she still in pain?"

Nurse Jesse fiddled with the bag attached to the tube in Gramma's arm. "The painkillers we gave her should be kicking in now. I'm sorry, Del, it might be a bit difficult to speak with her after all."

Del was going to ask to talk with the doctor who'd seen Gramma when another nurse entered holding a tablet. Nurse Jesse thanked her, then handed the tablet to Del. "Here. I'll give you some privacy."

Del took the tablet in her free hand. "Dad!" she shouted.

"Hi, sweetheart." Her dad was dressed in his physical training uniform, his white T-shirt visible under his blue-and-white reflective zip-up athletic jacket. His haircut was fresh, the lines all crisp. "How are you doing?"

"I'm okay. But Gramma isn't." She turned the tablet toward the bed so Dad could see her. Gramma made another sound she couldn't understand and reached toward the tray table. Del propped the tablet up by nestling it in the mounds of blankets on the hospital bed. Then she poured some of the water from the pitcher into the cup on the table, in case Gramma got thirsty.

"Yes, I spoke to Mama Violet already, and her doctor," her dad said, rubbing his palm over his face. "Look, Del—"

Del interrupted. "When are you coming home?"

"I said, listen."

"No, you said look."

Her dad groaned. "Well, I meant listen. I know your grandmother hasn't been doing great lately, but I wasn't expecting anything like this to happen, and well . . . I can't get back home right now."

Del let go of Gramma's hand and dropped into the chair next to her bed. "But . . . we need you!"

"I know." He sighed and leaned closer to the camera. "But this is a deployment assignment, Del. I can't just

33

leave. They'd have to process the entire squadron and pull us all out at once. It's tough to do that. Especially since this is my first time as CO. Training will take a few weeks, and I can't leave until it's over."

Del tightened her mouth into a hard line.

"I know this has been hard on you both," he continued. "Moving again, not having me around to help—"

"It *has* been hard," Del agreed. "But I've handled it. And if you can't get home yet, well, I can take care of Gramma until you get here."

"No, you can't."

Del mouth dropped open. "What do you mean?"

"I mean, your grandmother has had a medical emergency and I'm four thousand miles away. This is not an eleven-year-old's situation to handle."

"Then what are we supposed to do?"

"That's what I wanted to talk to you about," Dad said. "Someone else is going to be taking care of you."

"What? Dad, I don't need a babysitter. And I don't want to stay with some random family from the base."

"It's not someone from the base," Dad said. His mouth tightened into a thin line. "You're going to be staying with your great-grandmother."

Del froze. "Who?"

"Your great-grandmother. Your gramma's mom."

"Gramma has a mom? I mean, one who's real? I mean, still alive—"

34

"Yes, Del, your grandmother has a mother, I can promise you she's real." Dad gave her a funny look. "Gramma was the one who suggested you might stay with her, and I was able to speak with your great-grandmother myself a few minutes ago." He leaned back in his chair. "She has agreed to take care of you while Gramma is ill and I'm away."

"But why . . ." Del began, then fell quiet. She didn't know how to finish that sentence. Or, she had way too many ways to finish it. Why didn't she know she had a great-grandmother? Why hadn't Gramma mentioned her before? Not one time did she ever hear Gramma talk about her own family. Why had she kept it a secret?

But those questions would have to wait. She could tell by the sound of her father's voice there wasn't going to be any arguing this point. "Fine," Del said. "When is my great-grandmother getting here?"

Her dad looked away from the camera, like he was reluctant to voice what he was going to say next. "She isn't. You're going to her. Down to a place called Nemmine Island, off the coast of South Carolina. It's where Gramma's from. She grew up there."

"Are you serious?" Del leaped to her feet. "We just moved yesterday! And now I have to go somewhere else?"

"That's right. Your great-grandmother apparently runs a school, which is about to start its summer session. I know this isn't easy, but—"

35

"I have to go back to *school*?" Del's heart dropped into her stomach. Before starting at a new school in the fall, she'd have to go to *another* new school? "This is supposed to be summer vacation."

Dad frowned. She could tell he was sympathetic about the situation, but he had only so much patience. "I'm not sure what sort of school it is, but I'm sure there will be a lot you can learn while you're in South Carolina about where your family is from. About agriculture and local animals, and the lingering effects of enslavement that still affect our people today."

Of course Dad would say that. He was a huge history nerd. "But I don't even know this person."

"There isn't another choice here, Delphinia," he said, calling her by her full name, which meant he meant business. "I can't get home right now, there's no one there to take care of you, and you can't take care of yourself on your own. I don't know what you expect me to say. If someone from Child Protective Services or the police finds out you are in that house alone, they will take you away from me and your gramma and put you in a foster home. That is not an option. Do you understand?"

Del's mouth dropped open, but she couldn't say anything. Tears stung behind her eyes, but they didn't fall. Her heart banged in her chest. She hadn't thought of that. All she'd thought of was that she could do things herself: cook, wash clothes, buy groceries . . . She'd even buy vegetables and eat them! Del looked away from the screen and pressed the heels of her hands to her eyelids. Dad wouldn't want her to lose it and cry.

When he saw her tears threaten to fall, his expression and voice softened. "I'm sorry, sweetheart. I didn't mean to yell. I'm upset all this is happening when I can't get to you. I'm not crazy about the fact I'm sending you to stay with a person I didn't even know existed until your gramma told me a little while ago. Mea culpa."

Del cleared her throat. "Does that mean 'I'm sorry'?"

"Technically it means 'through my fault' in Latin, but yes. I'm so sorry."

They were quiet for a minute while she wiped her eyes and dragged in a shaky breath. She reached and took Gramma's hand in hers. She didn't stir, but her hand was warm.

"This isn't the ideal situation, Del. I recognize that." Her dad was talking again and Del forced herself to look back at the screen. "But I need to you handle this, like you handle everything else. Remember, in a few more years, I'll have my twenty in. Then I can retire and we'll all figure out what happens next, together. Okay?"

Del straightened her posture and nodded. "Yes, sir."

"That's my capable girl. Your gramma needs time to rest and recover, and in the meantime, I want to you to make the best of an unfortunate situation, like we always do. Be polite to your great-grandmother, listen to what she says, and we'll all be back together in no time."

Gramma's hand moved in Del's, giving it a light squeeze. She looked up to see Gramma watching her. She nodded, just barely, then leaned back on the stack of pillows.

"Okay," Del said. "I can do it."

A door opened behind her dad and another man in uniform peered inside. Her dad muted the audio, turned to the side, and spoke a few words. The other man nodded and closed the door as he left. When her dad pushed the button again to unmute the microphone, he was all business.

"I have to go, Del. Someone from the base will be coming to bring you from the hospital to the house. They'll stay with you tonight, and in the morning, they'll take you to the airport and see that you get on a flight to Charleston, South Carolina. Then someone will meet you there and drive you to where you'll meet your great-grandmother. I'm emailing you travel details. Be careful, text me along the way, and try to have some fun while you're there, okay?"

"Yes, sir," she said again.

"Love you, sweetheart."

"Wait, Dad!"

But he was already gone and the screen was blank.

When she gazed up, Gramma seemed to have fallen asleep again. Her breathing wheezed a little, but at least it was steady. People in white coats rushed by, but none of them came into the room. Already she felt alone. Without the only two people she loved and trusted. Del wished things were different, but she knew wishing didn't help anything. You couldn't wave a magic wand around and change the way life worked.

She gazed at the empty screen where her dad's face had been a moment ago. "Love you too."

4

It was hard for Del to believe it had been only a day since she'd been sitting in Gramma's hospital room. She was now waiting at the Atlantic Ocean shoreline somewhere in South Carolina, holding her rolling suitcase handle with her backpack on her shoulders and buckled around her waist.

Pauline, the recruit Dad had sent, had driven her from the hospital to their new home, and Del had immediately packed her things. It was strange to be digging through her big suitcase and boxes to find her clothes and shoes, only to pack them in a different, smaller suitcase for a trip she didn't want to go on. She added a couple of books to her suitcase too. Things could get real boring real quick when she got where she was going, especially if her great-grandmother was busy running a school all day. She might be left to entertain herself.

Once Del was packed and had double- and triple-checked everything, she fell into bed. Pauline slept downstairs on the sofa after Del had shown her where the extra pillows and blankets were. Even though she was exhausted, she had no idea how she was going to get any sleep. But she must have, because she'd had a horrible nightmare that shook her to her bones.

In a dark hospital, Del roamed the empty hallways. *Why is there no one here?* She shoved her hands deep in the pockets of her jeans, wishing she had a jacket. It was so cold she could see her breath. She peeked into some of the rooms, expecting to find at least one person who could tell her what was happening. But the place was deserted. Where was everyone?

Above her the fluorescent lights flickered, making Del quicken her steps through the hospital corridors, her footsteps echoing off the bare walls. Del rubbed her hands up and down her arms to warm them. Finally, she saw a light in the distance, cutting through the spooky dimness. She rushed toward it to find a long, brightly lit room. She sighed in relief at being able to stand in the light again. When she looked in the window, her relief slid away like a loosened scarf. Inside the room were rows and rows of small cribs. To her horror, they were all empty.

Except one.

Who would leave their baby? Del pressed her palm against the window, peering closer to see the name on the crib. When her vision adjusted, she could see the last name written in bold, block letters.

BAKER

Was that baby supposed to be her? She pulled the door handle to find it locked. She yanked and beat on the door, shouted and screamed for help, but no one came.

Del woke in a cold sweat, her entire body shaking as she struggled to sit up. Her throat was raw and irritated as if she had screamed in real life and not just in the dream. She panted as if she had run miles. She turned the pillow over to find a dry spot and lay down again. It was a long time before she settled enough to go back to sleep.

The next thing she knew, the sun was up. Pauline drove Del to the airport in Baltimore, where she got on a flight to Charleston. The plane ride wasn't long, but it was hard. On her right sat a smelly-footed man who kept wiggling his bare toes. Behind her, some kid kept kicking the back of her seat. By the time the airplane touched down two hours later, Del was a ball of frustration and completely grossed out. She waited until almost everyone else had gotten off the plane before she got up and asked the flight attendant to help her get her suitcase out of the overhead compartment. A man holding a sign with her name on it was waiting for her at the gate, a driver Dad had arranged to take her to meet her gramma's mother.

By the time Del had climbed into the back seat of the car with her suitcase and backpack, she was even more frustrated. She was already tired. She shouldn't be here; she should be with Gramma. The nightmare she'd had last night, on top all the worry and fear she'd accumulated over the past twenty-four hours, had transformed into irritation. Hadn't she always helped take care of Gramma and the house while Dad was away? What was different now? And this car was crawling along like the last few minutes of class at the end of the school day. Del had closed her eyes and willed the car to move faster. The waiting made her even more anxious.

After what felt like ages, the driver had pulled off the paved street onto a hard-packed dirt road, then another, and another, until they were suddenly at the edge of the water. Thick reeds and grasses grew along this edge and Del had to work to catch a glimpse of the water through the dense greenery. It was like someone wanted to hide it from view, until . . . poof! There it was.

Finally, the driver had parked the car and got out. Del followed, falling out of the car into a wall of heat like nothing she had ever felt before. The air was so thick, Del thought she could grasp it in her hand and squeeze.

Instantly, sweat beaded on her forehead. She stared at the endless rippling water in front of her. Small houses were scattered around, but she could only see their battered roofs. From the shoreline, it looked like she was standing on the last piece of dry land in the world. The new house in Delaware felt so far away.

The trunk of the car slammed and the driver placed her bags next to her.

Del took out her phone. "How much for the ride?"

"It's already paid, miss." He touched his beat-up baseball cap, and before she could respond, he was back in the air-conditioned car. In another few blinks, he was gone, a faint cloud of dust the only sign he had ever been there.

Now Del stood alone in this damp, dense heat that was draining her energy moment by moment. She couldn't stop thinking about Gramma, who was so sick, and yet, here Del was, on the edge of the world under the hottest sun in existence, waiting for some woman she'd never met before to pick her up.

Sweat dripped down her forehead and Del wiped it away with the back of her hand. She gathered up her braids and held them off her neck to get some relief. How did anyone live here? Mosquitoes buzzed in her ears, biting her faster than she could slap at them. Her jeans and T-shirt stuck to her skin. She dug in her suitcase for her sunglasses but came up empty. Had she forgotten to pack them? There was a single tree near the water's edge, and she leaned against it, happy for some shade. The only other plants surrounding her were short, scrappy bushes, fan-shaped leaves with thick stems, and spindly-looking patches of grass. She adjusted her backpack and lowered the pull handle of her rolling suitcase so she could sit on it.

Del hummed the melody to her gramma's song as she waited. How could she stand a few weeks of this? Already she didn't want to spend not another day in this place. In front of her was calm green-gray water. It ran as far as she could see, broken only by an occasional splash from a fish leaping up, then plunging beneath the surface. The fish's movement captured the attention of a passing bird, and it dove like an arrow into the ocean, then swooped up, rising into the sky with its wriggling catch and flying off until Del couldn't see it anymore.

Del leaned down to pick up a smooth, flat stone, and flung it into the water with all her might. It landed with a thunk and a splash, then ripples floated outward from where it sank into the ocean. Satisfied, she brushed the sand off her hands, confident she'd show her dad she could be of help, and he'd apologize for sending her down here and he'd—

The whirling rush of Del's thoughts came to an abrupt stop as a boat appeared on the water, gliding toward the shore. Del leaped to her feet, the suitcase toppling over behind her. That boat hadn't been there a second ago. Nothing except birds and fish were in that water—where had it come from? Del blinked, bringing the boat into focus under the almost blinding sunlight. It was a wooden boat, and didn't appear to have any sort of outboard motor. Still, it moved smoothly across the water. A figure stood in the middle of the small craft, but there were no paddles or oars, and Del wondered how it was moving all. Her shoulders tensed.

As the boat grew closer, she could see the person in the boat was an old woman. She stood tall and still as a statue, with her arms crossed in front of her. The boat rocked gently from side to side, but the woman didn't lose her balance.

Del had been so busy with packing, the plane ride, and the car trip, she hadn't really thought much about the fact that, for the first time in her life, she would be meeting a member of her family that wasn't Dad or Gramma. But looking this woman in the eyes, reality dropped inside her like the stone she had carelessly thrown in the ocean.

The woman wore a long-sleeved pale blue-and-white striped dress made from some sort of floaty fabric. Even with the long sleeves of the dress, not a drop of sweat showed on the woman's face. In one hand she held a walking stick of shiny polished wood, almost as tall as she was, that gleamed in the sunlight. Bright red cloth covered the place where the woman's hand rested. A sense of power and strength emanated from her, and for the briefest moment, Del caught a fleeting scent of cinnamon.

Del could see something familiar in the face of the woman floating toward her. The woman's hair was dark and coily like Del's but swept up in a high bun with a silvery gray streak in the front. They were a similar brown complexion. There was something in her expression Del recognized, though she couldn't put her finger on it.

She shook her head, remembering her dad's instructions. *Be polite. Be polite. Be polite.* The boat approached the shore, where Del expected it to come to a gradual stop. But it didn't. Instead, it lifted up from the ocean, water dripping from the bottom like a rubber duck plucked out of a bathtub.

Del's mouth fell open.

The biggest alligator she'd ever seen climbed up onto the shore, the boat on its back. It waddled up on the sand, through scrubby grasses, and crouched, waiting. The alligator had to be longer than the bus Del used to ride to school. She hoped it wasn't hungry. As if in response, the alligator opened its massive jaws wide. It snapped its teeth and swished its tail impatiently, but it didn't come any closer.

Del yanked her gaze away from the creature and found the woman looking her over from head to toe. Her eyes went from Del's waterfall of plaits that hung almost to her waist, down to her yellow "Braids Rule!" ringer T-shirt, then her jeans, and finally her white sneakers with the braided shoelaces.

The corners of the woman's mouth twitched up, and then she spoke. Her voice was smooth, the words crisp and tart as a green apple. "You must be Delphinia. How do?"

"Um, hi." She winced at the use of her full name; she hated it so much. None of the kids at any school she'd been to could even pronounce it right. "I like 'Del.'"

"Who is—oh, I see." The old woman nodded as if making a note to herself. "You prefer to be called Del." The woman held her shoulders back and her head high as she stepped backward in the boat. She was graceful as a queen, and her movements were like dance steps. "My name is Rose Vesey. I'm your grandmother's mother."

Even though Del knew the woman was her relative, hearing it was still a shock. "You're my Nana Rose?"

"Nana Rose," her great-grandmother repeated slowly, like she was testing out the title. "I like that." She patted the side of the wooden boat so it let out a hollow thump, then held out her hand. "Come on aboard."

"Is it . . ." Del eyed the reptile's massive jaw. The beast could probably snap her up in one mouthful. "Is it safe?"

Nana Rose raised her eyebrows. "Why wouldn't it be?"

Del blinked at her, then set her jaw and crept forward. Carefully, she placed her suitcase in the boat. The alligator stayed still for the most part, but one of its eyes rolled to follow her movements.

"That's Ol' Lundy—a legend around these parts. He won't bother you a bit." Nana Rose sat down and patted the alligator's massive tail. He let out a growl-sigh. "Unless you bother me, that is."

Del gulped. She'd seen a documentary once that said a young alligator could knock over a full-grown adult with a single swipe of its tail. She could only imagine what a gator like Lundy could do to a kid.

"Yeah, um. Don't worry, I won't." She took Nana Rose's hand, and with surprising strength, the woman tugged her aboard.

"Now that's settled." Del's great-grandmother smirked. "Let's go."

Ol' Lundy turned with surprising speed and slid soundlessly back into the water. Del shrugged out of her backpack and set it on the floor of the boat. Kisses of cool air soothed her overheated skin.

As they glided through the water, Del snuck glances at the woman beside her. Up close, she looked a lot younger than she must have been. Younger than Gramma, even.

"You don't look like a great-grandmother," Del said.

"And what does a great-grandmother look like?"

She hesitated. "Well, you know—"

"No, I don't know. That's why I asked." Nana Rose trailed her fingertips in the water. "It's important to ask when you don't know the answer to something."

No, I don't know. That's why I asked. The same words Del heard Gramma use just a few days ago. It was disturbing—like hearing an echo after too much time had passed.

Del looked closer at Nana Rose, trying to think of a response to her question. What *did* a great-grandmother look like? Del had never met a great-grandmother before, so how was she supposed to know? Nana Rose moved the glossy stick in her hand, turning it round and round in a circle until Del was dizzy looking at it.

" . . . Just old, I guess."

"Well, I am that."

"You're not angry? Or offended?"

Nana Rose laughed. "That you said I was old? It's true, isn't it?"

Del looked away from her warm gaze. "I guess."

"You said the words, better own 'em."

The boat glided through the water, only rocking slightly. Del wanted to brush her fingertips over the part of Ol' Lundy's wide greenish-brown back the boat didn't cover but the thought of that huge, powerful jaw filled with craggy teeth made her pause. She decided to change the subject. "My dad said you're a teacher?"

"Yes, I am. Most of my time these days is spent running our school, which is called the Vesey Conservatory. But I still teach sometimes."

"What do you teach?"

"The school specializes in teaching our people's history."

"'Our people'?"

Nana Rose nodded. "Yes. Sea Island people. Gullah

people. Like me and your grandmother and your mother, you are directly descended from enslaved Africans who built the rice, cotton, and indigo industries in this country. Many of our ways echo those found in West and West-Central Africa. Has Violet—your grandmother—told you anything about our family or this island?"

Del turned in the boat to look back at the shore. They'd drifted forward so easily that if she hadn't looked behind her, she would have thought they weren't moving at all. The land they had departed from was so far in the distance now she could barely see it. It felt as far away as her life with Gramma and Dad.

"No, she never said anything."

Del could feel in the boat's movements that Nana Rose had also turned. "My sincere apologies, Delphinia."

Instead of correcting the use of her full name, she faced forward and tugged at one of her braids. "Why are you apologizing?"

Nana Rose twisted the stick in her hands. "I'm sorry you weren't introduced to us before now. This place holds a part of your heritage." She pressed her lips together into a tight line as if she had more to say but wasn't sure if she wanted to.

But Del forged ahead. If Dad and Gramma wouldn't answer any questions about her family's history, maybe Nana Rose would. At least she would know about what Gramma had been like as a kid. "If heritage is so important, why would Gramma keep it from me?"

"If you're asking why your grandmother never spoke of her life growing up on Nemmine Island, or of me, I don't know her reasons." She waved a hand in the air, and it was a moment before Del realized she was shooing away bugs, so tiny Del could barely see them. "Maybe, when she's better, we can both ask her."

If Gramma had decided not to tell anyone her mom was still alive, why would she want to start talking about her now? The question kept nipping at her like a puppy that wanted attention. But it didn't seem like she was going to get an answer from Nana Rose after all. At least not yet. So she tried another question. "Do you know exactly what happened to Gramma? No one told me."

"Oh, dear. I'm sure it was an oversight on your father's part. So much happened in such a short time . . . Your gramma has appendicitis and needs to have surgery. Today. Her recovery will take some time, maybe three to four weeks."

Del blew out a long breath. She had hoped Gramma would recover much faster. Guess that wasn't going to happen. She fiddled with her backpack straps, loosening and tightening them. "So, how do you teach 'our people's history'?"

"We educate students in many of our cultural traditions." The breeze ruffled Nana Rose's long skirt and she adjusted it. "Did your grandmother ever teach you any rituals?"

"Rituals?" Del frowned. "That sounds creepy."

"Not necessarily. A ritual is simply something you do so often, you don't have to think about it." Nana Rose lifted her shoulders in a shrug. "They don't have to be creepy or strange or even take a long time. For instance, you know all those things you do every night to get ready for bed? That is your nightly ritual."

Del bit her lip. Did she and Gramma have any rituals? They had traditions like the ones they always did on moving-in day. And every spring, they planted tomato and cucumber seeds to harvest in the summer. At the start of each school year, they always went shopping for new clothes and shoes. She supposed those were rituals, but she wasn't sure she was ready to share any of that information. "Gramma and I have our own traditions we made up for ourselves" was what Del said.

Nana Rose nodded. "Well, we have a number of unique traditions and practices. You can learn about them while you're here."

"Like what?"

"What we teach has many names. Some call it 'Southern conjure,' or 'conjure magic.'" Nana Rose gave Del a gentle smile. "Have you heard of it?"

"Conjure . . . magic?" She looked at Nana Rose closely,

but couldn't tell if her great-grandmother was joking. She looked serious, even with the small curve on her lips.

"Yes, magic. Our people have been practicing it in this part of the world for over four hundred years."

"Oh," Del said, understanding now. "You're talking about things from back when people didn't know about science or whatever, and believed in magic. Not like, *actual* magic."

Nana Rose folded her hands in her lap. "What do you mean?"

Del didn't know how to say it any more clearly than that. "I mean . . . magic isn't real."

"What makes you say that?" Nana Rose asked, her voice calm and even.

"Because if it were, then . . ." She shrugged. "Well, then everyone would know about it."

"There are a lot of things we do here that many people don't know about or care to learn about," Nana Rose responded.

"Okay, fine," Del said, bewildered she was even having to explain this. "Well, if magic was real, then . . ." She let rest of what she was going to say drift away, not wanting to finish the sentence.

"Then?" Nana Rose's voice gently nudged her.

Del swallowed. "Did you teach this magic to Gramma?"

"Yes, I did."

"Then wouldn't Gramma have used that magic to stop my mom from dying?"

Del expected Nana Rose to look away, or mumble some apology like most people did when she mentioned her mom. Instead, something Del couldn't name crossed Nana Rose's face. Her slow exhale of breath surrounded Del with the sweet fragrance of warm sugar. "Conjure magic isn't like magic you may have seen in movies."

"That's what I thought." Del turned away to look at the water again.

But Nana Rose continued. "By that, I mean it doesn't keep every bad thing from happening."

Del picked at the luggage tag on her suitcase. "What's it good for, then?"

Nana Rose adjusted her grip on her walking stick, opening and closing her hand around the red cloth. "It connects people, builds community, and strengthens bonds. Among other things."

"What sorts of other things?"

"That's what I'm hoping you'll learn."

Del doubted it. She didn't have any interest in chanting, or Ouija boards, or whatever weird things they taught at this school. If she was unsure about this place before, she definitely knew she didn't want to be here now. What she wanted was to be back at the new house, with Gramma and Dad.

She trailed her hand in the water, but yanked it back almost immediately; it was hot as bathwater. The quiet slosh of Ol' Lundy's tail propelling them forward, the flapping of bird's wings accompanying their excited calls, the wind making tiny waves in the water—it was all so different from any other place she'd lived in her whole life.

It was also the first time she'd gone anywhere without Gramma or Dad with her. She'd have only herself to rely on. All while worrying if Gramma was going to be okay, or if she was only going to get sicker. And wondering when she'd be able to get back home.

Ahead of her, Del saw miles and miles of ocean without end. So far to go. And she wondered what other kinds of hot water she would be getting herself into this summer.

5

Ol' Lundy swerved to avoid a floating log and the movement made Del grasp the side of the boat to avoid toppling into the water. She hadn't spent much time in boats, and it was hard to keep steady on the alligator's back. Especially when her mind was in three different places: in the hospital with Gramma, on the other side of the world with Dad, and here on the way to an island with a relative she never knew existed.

It was all so weird—something that only happened in dreams. Or nightmares. She was going on a long, strange trip alone and she had no idea what people or places she'd encounter on the way. She shook her head, her braids smacking against her cheeks. Any minute now, she'd wake up in her own bed to the sound of Gramma sweeping the kitchen like she did every day.

But this was no dream. When she'd touched it, the warm water had been real. There was a damp patch on the knee of her jeans where she'd wiped her fingers. In the extreme heat, though, it was drying quickly. Disappearing. She wished magic actually was real, so she could disappear, and reappear back home with Gramma.

As the minutes dragged on, Del had to accept this was really happening. She and her great-grandmother sat in a boat on the back of an alligator bound for an island in the middle of the sea. For a long while neither one of them said anything, and the silence between them got heavier and heavier.

Finally, Ol' Lundy smacked his tail in the water, showering both Del and Nana Rose with a fine rain of warm ocean. It did the trick of jolting both Nana Rose and Del out of the uncomfortable stillness. Del looked over the side, and the gator was moving its great big head from side to side.

"Well, I guess he doesn't like too much tension," Nana Rose said, smoothing a stray coil of her hair into place.

"Me either," Del said.

Nana Rose folded her hands in her lap. "This must be a trying time for you, Del. So many things happening and you want to be where you feel you're needed. But one thing conjure magic is good at is connecting people. One way to connect with your grandmother when you can't be with her is to learn more about where she came from. What shaped her as a person. And if you want to know what life for your gramma was like at your age, this is the place."

She gestured with her hands like she was presenting the entire ocean to Del as a gift. "So when you see her again, you'll have a whole lot more to talk about. And a stronger bond with her than ever."

"That would be nice," Del replied, mostly to be polite. She couldn't imagine having a stronger bond with her Gramma than she already had. But since Gramma never talked about what her life was like as a kid maybe Del could learn something about her while she was here. One thing Del knew she could do was adjust. If she could move and start her life all over again every year, then she could manage staying on this island for a month.

"When are we gonna get there?" she asked, closing her eyes to block out the worst of the bright white sun. "Where is—"

"We're here," Nana Rose said.

Del spun around to look, rocking the boat and earning her a cautionary growl from Ol' Lundy. "Sorry," she said to the creature. No way did she want to get eaten by an alligator on her first day here. Or any day, to be honest.

The entire island seemed to emerge from the water as they made their way toward the wide expanse of golden sand. "Where did this place come from? It wasn't here a second ago."

"This is Nemmine Island, my home and the home of Vesey Conservatory," Nana Rose replied, her voice bright.

Del pulled out her phone to see if she could figure out exactly where they were. When Nana Rose saw her, she said, "You won't find it on any map. Seclusion is a big part of our way of life. It helps preserve our culture and our ways from the outside world."

Del scratched her head. "You mean the school doesn't have a website or anything? How do people even know the school exists?"

Nana Rose shifted in her seat. It was the first time Del noticed any sign she was uncomfortable. "We are the only school left in South Carolina teaching the traditional ways of Southern conjure. I will admit, it hasn't been easy to find students to fill our classes these past few years. But there are a few who want to learn or have their children learn. And we get by." Nana Rose looked like she wanted to say more, but appeared to think better of it. "Ah, home again."

Nana Rose stood, waiting until Ol' Lundy swam up to shore and crawled onto the pale beach before getting out. The place where they'd landed was a wide expanse of off-white sand, edged with long grasses that waved in welcome. A few tall palm trees rustled their leaves, far above their heads. Waves sloshed against the shore, soaking the sand and turning it the color of toast.

"Come, the school isn't far. I'll help you with your bags." Nana Rose's heels crunched on the gritty sand.

"No, thank you," Del said as she pocketed her phone. "I've got 'em."

"Okay. Thank you, Lundy," Nana Rose said, turning to walk up the path between the toasty sand and the sprinkling of grasses at the water's edge.

Del lugged her backpack and suitcase out of the boat, somehow managing not to fall onto her butt. "Ugh," she complained when the sweat-dampened fabric of her shirt was once again pressed against her skin.

Ol' Lundy made a huffing, snuffling sound.

"What are you looking at?" Del snapped.

The gator opened his mouth wide, showing once again his two rows of massive teeth, and hissed. Del shrieked and ran to catch up with Nana Rose, the sound of the alligator's tail thumping the sand following her.

Nana Rose walked along the bendy path through the trees. Del, following close behind, was breathing hard by the time they stopped walking, and she gratefully plonked herself down on the edge of her suitcase for a rest.

But Nana Rose didn't look bothered at all. "Here we are!"

Del stared at the old house at the top of the path where Nana Rose had stopped. She wasn't sure what she'd expected, but it wasn't this. *What a dump.*

The tiny house looked like she could blow it over. The boards making up the house were rotted and crumbling, leaving open holes. All the grass was overgrown and turning brown. Bits of old tires and empty buckets lay decaying on the ground. This place needed a ton of repairs before anyone could even think of living in it. If it could even be fixed at all.

"This is your school?" Del flipped her braids over her shoulder. Disappointment crept into her voice, and she was too tired to hide it. No wonder her great-grandmother didn't advertise online. No one would ever come here if they saw a picture of this place. Del wasn't sure how they got any students at all. Her gramma grew up *here*?

Nana Rose twirled the wooden stick in a circle with the fingers of her left hand. "Welcome to Vesey Conservatory for the Wonder Arts."

"The 'wonder arts'?" Del scoffed. She supposed it sounded a little more believable than "magic." Still, she couldn't believe that *someone* wouldn't have posted about this place online. She pulled out her phone to check.

"Sorry, but you won't be able to use that here," Nana Rose said, not looking one bit sorry.

Del peered at the screen. No signal. She lifted her phone high above her head, hoping at least one bar would appear. "Are you serious? Why not?"

"Almost two hundred years ago, our ancestors who were enslaved on this island overthrew their captors and exiled them. Afterward, they constructed a barrier to hide the island from anyone with intentions to harm us and our way of life. It's tradition to preserve the work of those original conjurers, some of whom gave their lives for our freedom. So we reinforce those boundaries, every year. The barrier blocks things like cellular signals."

Del blinked. She couldn't believe this! "How do you contact people when you need to? I mean, what if I need to talk to my dad? Or check on Gramma?"

"We have ways of contacting those not on the island, which I will share with you. I spoke with your father and your grandmother, didn't I?" Nana Rose commented.

Great. Any time she wanted to see how Gramma was doing, she'd have to ask for permission to use the phone. "How do you even live out here, cut off from everything?"

Nana Rose straightened. "We have a rich, fulfilling life."

She took a deep breath, and held it long enough that Del got a bit worried, before exhaling. Del realized she had no idea what to do if Nana Rose just fell over. Her heart thudded in her chest at the memory of Gramma collapsing and how helpless she'd been. It was all so fresh in her mind. And now her phone was useless. What would she do if Nana Rose really was in trouble, and she couldn't call for an ambulance like she had with Gramma? What if she needed to talk to Dad, and there wasn't anyone around to let her use the island phone?

"You don't understand. I *need* my phone."

Nana Rose made a sound not unlike Ol' Lundy's hiss. "Well, then the next few weeks are going to be a little difficult for you."

A huge weight fell on Del's shoulders. She groaned and shifted her backpack to ease the ache from carrying it. But the achy weight wasn't only her backpack. It was the feeling of one more thing going wrong. One more thing outside of her control.

Del took in the rest of the scene around them. There was little else except the rustle of leaves in the low-hanging trees, blowing dirt, and the wind snapping the fabric of Nana Rose's dress. Del glanced up into the branches of the tree they'd stopped under. The limbs were long and stretched out and some kind of hairy stuff draped over each branch like scraps of worn fabric. Weird.

Del's skin prickled and her hair was like a carpet lying on her back. She didn't like this place. When Del looked up, Nana Rose was observing her with an odd expression: like uncertainty, determination, and hope all mixed together.

What else could she do? Del straightened her back. "So . . . I'm here, what now?"

"Now it's time for a cookout," Nana Rose said with a smile. "We are people with a culture of connections made by sharing food and drink. Tomorrow is the official start of our yearly summer session where potential students meet each other and the sorcells—that's what we call our teachers—and learn some of the history of Southern conjure magic. Sometimes, we even manage to get in a few basic lessons." Nana Rose glanced over at Del. "It helps students decide if they want to return for a full year."

"So, I'm going to meet a bunch of new kids?" Del groaned. "And a bunch of teachers?"

"You are." Nana Rose nodded. "After that, I'll show you where you'll be staying, give you a little tour of the house, just the two of us. We only have a short time to get to know each other."

"We have almost a month. That's a long time."

"Not when I've been waiting your whole life to meet you," Nana Rose said, passing her walking stick from one hand to the other.

"Um, Nana Rose . . ." Keeping in mind her promise to her father to be polite and learn all she could, Del took a deep breath. "For as long as I can remember, it's been me, my dad, and my gramma. And we've been doing fine, just the three of us. And now all of a sudden, I'm being told all this new stuff. I have a great-grandmother, and this whole family history, and 'people' and 'heritage' and 'connections' and, well . . ." Del threw her hands up in the air. "Gramma didn't think I needed to know about any of this, otherwise she would have said something sooner."

Shoulda told you, baby.

The words her gramma said to Del in the hospital

came flying back into her memory. Had Gramma been talking about Nana Rose and Nemmine Island? There was no way to know. But even if it was, why would she have waited until then to tell her?

"Delphinia, I'm not sure—"

"It's just Del," she corrected.

"Del. This is a lot to handle, especially when you'd rather be with your grandmother. But I'm sure she'd feel better knowing you were being taken care of while she recovers. Besides, joining us for classes must be more fun than sitting in your room all day, with no working phone."

Del had to admit she was right about that. She took a deep breath. "Fine. But can you not introduce me as your great-granddaughter? I'm not . . ." She wasn't sure how to finish the sentence and her voice trailed off.

"You're not comfortable with it?"

"Exactly."

"In that case, you may call me Sorcell Rose as the others do, and I will introduce you as a last-minute addition to the summer session." She raised an eyebrow. "How does that sound?"

"It sounds fine. Thank you."

"Now that's settled, let's continue on. I'm sure you must be hungry after your trip."

The cookout, at least, sounded good. The single bag of dry pretzels she ate on the airplane was so long ago and Del was looking forward to a real meal. She nodded.

Nana Rose headed toward the run-down house again. Her back was straight as a pole and the shells dangling from her earlobes flashed golden white in the sun. She seemed to glide instead of walk, but her feet did strike the ground, softly as if she tiptoed on clouds. Trudging after her great-grandmother, Del lugged her suitcase along the bumpy, uneven ground until the path smoothed out as they neared the rickety old house.

"We'll take your bags to your room later, but for now you can put them on the porch there, then follow me across the front lawn."

In the distance, Del could hear voices, upbeat and fun, and faint laughter. The scent of a charcoal barbeque grill reached her and she inhaled deeply. Her stomach rumbled as she smelled the mixture of foods, none of which she could identify specifically. It all smelled so good. At least the food might be all right here.

It's only for a few weeks, she told herself. *You've moved tons of times before. This won't be any different. Would it?*

6

Del tramped along after Nana Rose, her steps somehow still falling farther and farther behind. Even freed of the burden of her bags, she couldn't keep up with this old woman's stride. Del noticed she didn't actually lean on her stick to help her walk; it was more like a friend holding her hand while they strolled along together.

The air surrounding Del was like steam from a hot cup of tea when you breathed it in: scented and moist. It was almost difficult to breathe. But Nana Rose didn't seem to be having any trouble. With a little jog, Del caught up to her. But when she pulled alongside the old woman, she didn't acknowledge Del's presence at all.

Del felt a little bad about what she'd said to Nana Rose. Not that she regretted it exactly. But she was more confused than ever about this person, this island, this place where Gramma grew up and never bothered to mention even when Del asked. Did Gramma really have a whole life here that she never once cared to tell Del about? Could Gramma have really known her own mother was alive this whole time, and never wanted to talk to her or visit her? If Del's mom was alive, she would want to see her as much as possible.

And even though Del knew Gramma must have had her reasons for not mentioning this island, she was still super curious.

"So do you own this whole island?"

"As far as you can see belongs to me, and to this school. It's been in our family for generations."

Del shaded her eyes with her hand. "As far as I can see is a lot."

If you ignored the main house and the land around it, the island was beautiful. A sea of deep green grass, neatly trimmed, led away from the house until it sank into a forest of blooming flowers off to the left. Behind her, the grass on the other side of the path ran down to the pale sand beach she came in on. To her right was a massive field, full of what looked like different varieties of corn and other plants. She'd never lived near any sort of farm, but she'd seen a few horror movies, and she knew that cornfields were never a good thing.

Sitting in the middle of it all, though, was an enormous white cloth tent, shaped like a pyramid, nestled on the far side of the lawn. Beside it was one of the biggest trees Del had ever seen. Some of its branches stretched wide and low to the ground, low enough for people to sit on them like chairs, and a few people were. Others were gathered in the shade of its taller branches, talking or playing. A few barbeque grills sizzled, emitting summer scents of charcoal and fire that made Del's mouth water.

But despite her hunger, the shouts of kids sent her stomach churning with nervousness. It was exactly the way she felt on every first day of school in a new city. Del swallowed the feeling down, like she always did. Maybe she could even find someone normal to hang out with. If she could, it might make the weeks here less boring.

Del and Nana Rose arrived at the low and wide tree, where three girls in white shirts and pink polka-dotted shorts were jumping double Dutch. Their heads were shaved smooth and their dark skin shone in the sunlight that filtered through the leaves. The grass was thinner here, and a rustling sound came from their white canvas slip-ons, keeping perfect time to the swish of the twirling ropes.

"Hello, girls," Nana Rose said, smiling. "Enjoying the shade?"

They stopped playing and stood completely still. Then, all at once, the three of them turned their heads. All their faces were exactly the same. Triplets.

"Hello, Sorcell Rose," they chorused. "Yes, we are."

"Girls, this is Del. She's just arrived, and is going to be with us for the summer program." Nana Rose nodded at the trio. "Del, these are Taye, Faye, and Kaye."

The girls turned again as one, in their wind-up toy way, and looked at Del, unblinking. Then they nodded to her. "How do you do?" they all said.

"Um, fine." *Which one is which?*

Nana Rose didn't make that clear. Instead, she placed her hand on Del's shoulder and the touch surprised her so much she nearly jumped out of her skin.

"Enjoy the cookout, girls," she said.

Nana Rose moved off toward the tent and Del trotted behind her, staying closer than she had before. As they approached the tent, the two adults underneath it, one woman and one man, watched them.

"Hello, sorcells," Nana Rose said.

They greeted her. "Sorcell Rose."

"This is our final new student of the year, Del Baker."

"Hello," Del said.

"We're glad to have you with us, Del." A voice like

71

gentle ocean waves rolled over her, and Del felt the tension of the trip melt away. "I'm Sorcell Nyla."

Her smile was warm and Del couldn't help but return it. "Nice to meet you," she said.

Sorcell Nyla sat in a wheelchair, a thin woven yellow blanket covering her from waist to toes. Her shoulders were straight and high, and her head was wrapped in a pale green scarf embroidered with gold that matched her blouse and concealed every inch of her hair. At least, Del guessed she had hair; there was no way to tell for sure. Around each wrist was a bracelet made of wood, polished smooth, surrounded by short, dark, stubbly hairs. It looked like someone had turned the boar bristle hairbrush Del used inside out and wrapped it around the sorcell's wrists.

Nana Rose had introduced the man next to Sorcell Nyla as a sorcell as well, but Del couldn't understand how he was a teacher here. Or anywhere, for that matter. He looked dirty and his clothes were torn and ripped. His hair and beard were out of control, overgrown and ratty. Cobwebs threaded throughout his inky beard, turning it a dusty gray, and his hair needed a pick and a line up. The only thing that looked decent was the cane made of deep brown polished wood that hung by its head from his belt.

He nodded in her direction. "I'm Sorcell Harus. Welcome, Del. To the island, and to Vesey Conservatory."

Surprisingly, his voice was clear and had a kind tone.

She returned Sorcell Harus's nod, still unsure of this disheveled man standing between two elegant, well-dressed women.

"I like your shirt," Sorcell Nyla said to Del.

Del laughed, finally feeling a little less nervous. "Thanks, I made it. With my gramma's help."

"Then you are talented and creative. Good qualities for a student."

Embarrassed by the compliment, Del changed the subject. "What do you both teach?"

Her great-grandmother said, "Harus teaches ancestral lore. Nyla teaches divinations and apotropy."

Del's head spun. "What are those classes? I've never learned anything about—"

A chime rang out like a church bell, cutting off Del's words.

"Time to kick things off. Gather 'round, everyone!" Nana Rose called. She strode to the middle of the lawn and tapped the ground with her stick.

A shoosh of cool wind blew through the area, nudging Del toward the group of students lining up to face the sorcells. Another girl, about her age, grinned at her as she took the place next to Del in line. She was shorter than Del, and had lighter brown skin and a head full of short, reddish-brown coils that looked painted in the sunlight. The girl also had a notebook opened to a page with a picture of a huge mansion drawn on it in pencil.

"Did you draw that? It's really good."

The girl nodded, then swallowed before answering. "Sorry, braces," she explained. "It's just a sketch, but thanks."

Del didn't know the difference between a drawing and a sketch, but she didn't have time to ask because the girl tucked the sketchbook under her arm as Nana Rose called for the group's attention.

"Welcome all, to the start of our summer session."

Kids shimmied around, trying to get the best view of Nana Rose, and she waited for them all to be still again before she continued. "While our staff is reduced in numbers over the summer, I know I speak for myself and our sorcells in attendance that we're happy to have you here for an introduction to Southern conjure and the wonder arts."

Everyone clapped. Were all the kids here actually into this conjure stuff too, whatever it was? She crossed her arms in front of her chest and frowned.

"As your instructors here at the Vesey Conservatory for the Wonder Arts, we are united in our ambition to inspire you to achieve and excel as you learn the ways and traditions of our people. It is our responsibility to keep this knowledge from being lost—to time, to neglect, to hostility. That's where our motto comes from: Protect, Educate, Survive. As a Vesey student, you aren't just joining a school—you're joining a community."

Del could hear the pride in Nana Rose's voice. Her shoulders were straight, her head was high, and her words were welcoming. Excitement floated through the gathered crowd.

"We are not always understood by those outside our community," Nana Rose continued. "Many don't accept or believe in what we do. But here, we respect each other's differences and celebrate all of our community's successes. This island is safe for self-expression, which will allow you to be fearless in your pursuit of knowledge, despite our difficult history."

Nana Rose motioned the other two sorcells forward and they joined her. "We keep this course small so we can give you personalized attention should you need it. If you already have some knowledge of conjure, we can help you grow. Even if you don't have any skills yet, you too can learn something during this session, if you're willing to work."

Sorcell Nyla spoke then, in a bright and bubbling voice. "We realize the transition from mainstream school to this conservatory can be stressful. This summer program can help to introduce you to our way of life and our way of conjuring, preparing you to meet the challenges ahead."

Del wondered what she meant. Was the schoolwork going to be especially hard? When she glanced around at the other students again, no one seemed to be worried. She felt an eagerness from the group that was hard to ignore. And the few students she'd met seemed friendly enough, although the triplets were a bit weird. Maybe the next month might not be as bad as she feared.

Then Del thought of Gramma in that hospital bed. What if she needed a drink of water or some medicine or something? Was Nurse Jesse there to take care of her? She instinctually reached into her pocket for her phone before remembering it was useless.

"I urge you to make the most out of this opportunity. To learn, to experience new things," Sorcell Harus said. "You are here to study, of course—that is the main focus of our program. But I hope you will also take time to enjoy each other's company outside the classroom. Many students establish friendships here that last a lifetime."

The girl with the notebook nudged Del in the side, bringing her out of her thoughts, and gestured with her eyes to Del's arm. Something trailed across her skin: a bright green caterpillar. She touched her finger to the path the creature was taking, letting it crawl on. Del kneeled down and placed the tiny insect on the grass, where it soon vanished into the rest of the crisp lawn. When Del stood, a flash of sunlight blinded her for a moment. She almost lost her footing and stumbled, but she managed to keep her balance.

"Again, welcome." Nana Rose tapped her stick on the ground, and a gentle vibration ran through the crowd, signaling the speech was over. Everyone clapped. Then Nana Rose stepped aside.

Sorcell Nyla rolled forward. "Let's work a little conjure right now, shall we? Join hands with the person beside you. We're going to recite a protection spell to keep us safe for the summer. It's an old spell that has been on the island for centuries and it sometimes needs refreshing. I can think of no better people to help us do that."

All the students and sorcells formed a circle and joined hands. The red-haired girl next to Del took her right hand while Del slipped her left into one of the triplets' firm grasp—Taye or Faye or Kaye, she didn't know which. She watched the other kids for any sign that one of them thought this was all as weird as she did, but they all had their eyes closed.

"Protect is the first tenet—or rule—of this conservatory's motto," Sorcell Nyla stated, her soft voice breezing sweetly throughout the group. "We are all special and important, and we must protect ourselves and our way of life from those who wish to destroy or discredit us. You'll begin to learn this now."

With that, the sorcell closed her eyes as well. "Please repeat after me so we can use our combined strength for this spell of protection."

While Del watched, Nyla spoke and all the students and sorcells repeated each line after her, like a chant:

Gold and silver, salt and sun
Keep us safe from outside harm.
Earth and air, water and time
Shield us all, and ease our minds . . .

Del watched everyone as they spoke but couldn't bring herself to say the words. *This is silly.* Del looked around as the chant continued. There was nothing else out here besides the tent, and the gardens bordering the woods, and the quiet lapping of the water against the docks. Who did they need protecting from? The mainland was a long boat ride away, and according to Nana Rose, the island wasn't on any maps. And who would want to come to this run-down place anyway? Then the sorcell clapped her hands sharply three times, signaling the end of the protection spell. The students on each side of Del released her fingers.

"Finally! Let's have some food!" Sorcell Harus called.

Everyone, including Del, laughed. The spell thing was weird, but if that was the only sort of "magic" she'd have to deal with, maybe it wouldn't be that bad.

The other students ran off in every direction around her, eventually ending up at the various grills and tables of food. Happiness and enjoyment filled the air. Slowly and with the tiniest smile on her face, Del followed. If she had to be on this island, she should at least get something good to eat.

7

As she strolled toward the cookout's many tables, Del passed the grills, covered with corn on the cob, skewers of shrimp, and vegetable kabobs. Her mouth began to water, and she marveled at the perfectly straight grill marks the food wore.

But before she could choose something to eat, Del felt eyes watching her.

She whipped around. No one appeared to be looking her way, but she knew that feeling of being watched carefully. All new kids did. Once she learned it was usually because her clothes or hair were different from what the kids at a particular school wore, or that she spoke with a different accent than the people in the town she was living in were used to, the stares became easier to ignore. But she still noticed it, every time.

As Del scanned the crowd, she saw the girl with the notebook who had stood beside her during Nana Rose's speech. She spotted Del as well and smiled wide, showing a mouth full of gold-colored braces which glinted in the sun.

"Hi, I'm Eva," she said, coming over to where Del stood under a tree near one of the charcoal grills. She shook Del's hand, pumping it up and down three times before releasing it.

"I'm Del," she said. "Do you always shake hands?"

Eva nodded, rubbing her short cap of tight reddish-brown curls. "My mom does it at her store. Says it's professional."

"But we're kids."

"Oh, I know," Eva said. "I'm practicing for when I am a professional conjurer. I don't know if I'll open my own store like my mom, though. I think more and more of the magic business will go online soon."

Eva was clearly into this conjure magic thing too. Del decided that to get along with everyone here, she'd have to go with it. It wasn't all that different from moving to a new town and learning how to act so she didn't stand out. "Did your mom go to school here?"

"Yep, she graduated a long time ago. Like, fifteen

years." Eva fanned herself with her sketchbook and the air circled around Del too. It wasn't much cooler but at least the air was moving instead of laying on her like a heavy blanket. "What about your mom? Does she practice conjure?"

Del rubbed her foot against the grass, letting the fresh green scent emerge. "My mom died giving birth to me."

"Oh, I'm really sorry," Eva said softly. "Maybe you can learn a way to connect with her while you're here."

"Um, yeah, that would be cool."

Part of her wondered why she told Eva about her mom. That was something she didn't usually like to share. But Eva's eyes sparkled and there was something about her that Del liked immediately. Eva was clearly happy to be here; maybe some of her energy would rub off on Del.

"We have a lot of studying to do first," Eva said. "I'm ready for it, though. Excited, y'know?"

Del didn't, but she nodded anyway. "Want to get a water ice?" she asked Eva, changing the subject.

Eva blinked. "A what?"

"Over there." Del pointed to a group of kids fishing cups of frozen, brightly colored fruit juices from a cooler. "Maybe something to cool down before getting some barbeque?"

"Oh, you mean a chilly bear. Sure! Race ya!" Eva darted off toward the cooler of iced treats. Surprised at how fast the girl moved in her buckled-up sandals, Del rushed to catch up.

As they waited in line, Del said, "What did you call these again?"

"Chilly bears."

"I've never heard that before. It's weird."

Eva gave Del a look she couldn't name. "You called it a water ice. I've never heard it called that before, but I didn't tell you it was weird." Her voice was careful, like she was trying to say something important—or *not* say something. "Might not be what you're used to, but that doesn't make it weird. Just different." She shrugged. "That's all."

"I . . . I'm sorry." The line moved and both of them took a few steps forward, closer to the coolers. "I didn't mean anything by it."

"I know. 'Cause I woulda read you if I thought you were being mean on purpose." Eva grinned again, and a lightness returned to the air around Del. "There's gonna be a lotta new and different stuff for us here. If we want to learn about it, we have to give it a chance."

"Maybe. But everything here is so . . . different." Del bit her lip. "Everything feels new. I'm not sure I can handle—" Del caught herself. She didn't want to admit that she felt lost already. She wanted something—anything—to feel normal right now. But Eva's open, smiling face invited her to be honest in a way she usually wasn't, and she didn't want to push away the first girl who was really nice to her since . . . well, ever. "I'm not sure I can handle all this . . . newness. It's a lot."

Eva nodded. "I'll tell you what my mom tells me when I get uncomfortable with something new." Her golden braces flashed. "If you wanna hear it, I mean. My mom's always got advice."

"Sure," Del said, entranced by Eva's singsong way of speaking. It was so musical when she talked, it reminded her of how Gramma spoke in the old interviews she gave when her song came out years ago. Del had seen the videos online when she searched for her grandmother's name and "Not Another Day" one time. Even though the picture quality was grainy, she liked it so much she'd bookmarked the video and watched it all the time.

Eva pointed to Del's sneakers, which had laces braided through the holes and tied in a double bow to keep them from unraveling. "You tie your own shoes?"

"Um, yeah."

"But you couldn't always do that, right? You had to learn." Eva tugged her ear. Del noticed the girl's earlobes were pierced, but she didn't have earrings in. Instead, her earlobes had short pieces of what looked like straw through them where the earrings should be.

"Yeah," Del said, slowly.

Eva twisted the bit of straw in her left ear, then the one in her right. "At first, it probably looked really hard, and someone had to show you how. And for a while, you couldn't do it. Then you tried and tried and one day, you could. Now you can do it without thinking."

They were almost at the front of the line. A boy had just scooped three frozen ices and was carrying them in both hands, all the cups pushed together in a triangle.

"I never thought about it like that."

Eva rose up on her tiptoes to see the colors of frozen ice in the coolers.

"I kinda like the name 'chilly bear,'" Del said. "It's cute."

"I like 'water ice.' It's two things that are the same, only, well . . . different." Eva laughed.

Del shoved her hands in her pockets and curled her toes inside her sneakers. If Eva was trying to help her feel like she belonged here, it wasn't quite working. Still, Del appreciated the effort. "Yeah, it is."

Eva chose lime and Del chose cherry. Both girls moved to the edge of the lawn, near the gardens, to lean against the lower branches of the old live oak tree. Del licked her chilly bear and showed Eva her red-stained tongue.

"This is so good and cold. I felt like I was melting before," Del said.

"I'm from here, and even I'm not used to heat like this." Eva laughed and sucked the flavor from a section of her chilly bear, turning it from green to white.

"You're from Nemmine?"

"Not from this island, but from Charleston, yeah."

"You don't sound Southern."

"That's probably because most Southern people don't

sound like they do in the movies. Most of those actors aren't really Southern and can't do the voice right." Eva made a face and changed her voice to make the words really long. "Theeeeyyyy ahhllllll sounnnnnd lahhhhk thiiiiiisss."

Del snorted with laughter. "You're right. Looks like you already taught me something."

"You did too."

Del turned back to the tent. Everyone was having a good time. Some kids were standing and eating by the grill, others were climbing the big wide tree, and a few were playing with rackets while they argued over who was going to set up a badminton net. She looked over to Nana Rose, who stood in the middle of the perfectly trimmed lawn, frowning up at the sky. The wind danced with the fabric of her skirt, but Nana Rose didn't seem to notice. A stab of cold went down Del's back that had nothing to do with the frozen treat.

Something was wrong.

A flurry of black birds darted through the air, swooping down twice, and then rising up into the sky. Her great-grandmother was watching the flight of the birds, the look on her face turning from concentration to concern. She whirled around, the hem of her dress blowing back in the wind. The fabric cracked and snapped like a flag in a storm. Del held her breath, her heart drumming behind her ribs.

Nana Rose gripped her walking stick by the red cloth around it and raised it high, then brought the end of it down hard onto the ground. Del's mouth fell open in astonishment. The top of Nana Rose's walking stick was changing. Where there had been nothing a moment ago, stick-straight bristles in rainbow colors now grew. They were as long as Del's forearm. In the space of a blink, the previously bare walking stick now wore a full head of multicolored bristles, bound tightly together with what looked like leather braid.

Nana Rose pounded the earth again and a vibration raced through the ground like a pulse, coming up through the soles of Del's feet, making her knees tremble, her heart race, and her teeth clatter in her mouth.

"Sorcells, to brooms!" Nana Rose yelled.

8

At Nana Rose's words, grunts and squeals erupted from the surrounding gardens. The ground rumbled and quivered like an earthquake.

"Harus, protect the students," Nana Rose shouted over the growing noise. "Nyla, with me." She rushed toward the sound faster than Del expected, Sorcell Nyla following close behind.

Sorcell Harus's voice was a gritty bark as he waved the students to stand next to him. "Here! Gather together," he urged, running toward the giant tree. All the kids clustered behind him as best they could.

He lifted the cane from his belt and swirled it around

his head. The dark wood whistled high and long, sprouting a fan of bristles the color of beach sand. A chocolate-brown cord emerged, wrapping around and around them before pulling tight. As Del watched, a stream of pinkish-red dust emerged from the bristles of the broom cane's orbit, encircling the students with a hovering line of fine powder. It looked like the ring around Saturn she'd seen in her science textbook. Within the circle of brick-colored dust, a few larger pieces hovered. Del reached her trembling fingers toward the space right under the orbiting rocks and powder. The moment her fingertip brushed against a fragment of pinkened rock, a force nudged her hand back.

"Don't touch it!"

Del jerked her hand away at the sorcell's sharp words. He was on high alert, watching the space where Nana Rose and Sorcell Nyla waited, facing outward toward the gardens and the woods. Leaves and branches shook, and the ground shuddered and vibrated.

"Easy, everyone," Nana Rose shouted. "They know we're aware of them. Once they—"

At that moment, a horde of snarling wild boars burst from the cover of the bushes and thundered toward the pair of sorcells. They were huge, covered in dark, bristly hair, with thick white tusks curling up from their jaws.

"Don't panic!" Nyla shouted above the pounding of hooves. "Our protection spell should stop them at the edge of the lawn."

Del gulped. Fear ran though her, making the sweat on her skin turn cold. She hadn't said the protection spell with the others. Surely one person not repeating the words wouldn't put everyone in danger. Right?

The lead boar, with its wicked-looking tusks, crashed through the tent at the edge of the property. It tossed its head back as it ran, throwing up the stakes holding it in place. After it, the other boars charged.

"The spell isn't holding! Take them!" Nana Rose shouted. She pounded her stick into the ground again and a transparent barrier like a large soap bubble rose from the grass, enclosing three of the boars. They threw their bodies against it, growling, snarling, and squealing.

Sorcell Nyla plucked individual straws from her bracelet and tossed them toward the stampede. Del didn't know what she thought those thin bits of straw would do against a charging boar. But as she watched, each straw widened as they all shot through the air, forming into darts that struck the ground in front of the stampede. From those darts, a wooden cage sprung up that enclosed the pigs. They battered their tusks against it, but the trap held.

Faster than a snake strike, Nana Rose threw her broomstick like a spear. As it hit the ground, the grasses sprung up to envelop some of the boars, tangling them up in dense weeds and vines until they couldn't move. She raised her empty hand and the broom wiggled its way out of the earth and returned to her.

"Is it over?" Del said to Eva, trembling.

"No," she said. "Look!"

The lead boar was still loose. It galloped on powerful legs, tusks down to attack, straight toward where Sorcell Nyla's wheelchair was positioned. Del gasped, tried to push through the circle to help the woman. But Sorcell Harus held out his hand to stop her.

"She can handle this," he said, a flash in his eyes.

Sure enough, Sorcell Nyla held her arms straight out in front of her body and brought her wrists together, her bracelets clattering. A rush of water erupted from where her hands met, lifting the animal up off the ground and washing it back into the woods from where it came.

Her hand over her mouth, Del gazed out at the destruction of the school grounds. Before the wild boars, the yard had been flawless and beautiful. Now thick tufts of grass were torn up from the monstrous creatures' trampling hooves. Deep holes littered the ground. The tent and the chairs were all knocked over and crushed. The charcoal from the overturned barbeque grills had singed spots in the grass. Anything the boars hadn't destroyed had been toppled by the other students in their rush to safety. Food littered the ground and birds flocked down to feast on it.

But something else had changed too. Del looked behind her, up toward the house, and she gasped, staggering back a step.

The run-down old shack she'd seen on her way to the

cookout had vanished. In its place was a massive white mansion. Even looking at the house from this distance made Del feel small. Four houses the size of the one she and Gramma had just moved into could easily fit inside. Behind the huge house, she could see more flashes of white if she lifted up on her tiptoes. Were there more buildings, or perhaps wings branching off from the main house? How big was this place?

She looked over at where Nana Rose stood surveying the damage. Tiny white shells and multicolored gems were woven into the bristles of Nana Rose's broom, and the whole thing glittered under the sunlight. The broom that had grown out of the cane Sorcell Harus held was decorated as well, the stones and crystals among the bristles humming. Del hadn't questioned the glittering of Sorcell Nyla's bracelets before, but now they vibrated with some unseen power.

Del sat down hard on what was left of the dense lawn. This magic, whatever it was, was real. She could see that. Before now, magic was something she read about in a book for fun, then forgot about when she moved on to the next one. There was nothing she had ever seen or heard in her entire life that could have told her otherwise. And yet, here it was.

Del's head spun. Was this the conjure her great-grandmother claimed their family had been practicing for centuries? Did it only work here on this island, and what was going on with those brooms? But while Del had a million questions, she didn't know how to ask any of them. How could she ask Nana Rose when she'd spent the last hour with her being so salty about coming to this island at all? Not to mention all the times she dismissed the word 'magic' . . . Nana Rose must be laughing at her right now. Or, she would be, if she wasn't dealing with all the damage the wild boars had done.

Despite her shock and awe and amazement at what she had witnessed, more than anything else, Del felt guilty. All she could think about was that she hadn't taken part in the protection spell. And now, the whole lawn was destroyed.

The sounds of others around her eventually pulled her out of her daze. Del watched as the other kids helped clean up the damage, and the sorcells used their brooms to magically lift the bamboo cages into the air and take the captured pigs back into the woods. A heavy weight settled on her neck and shoulders. The kind a person got from someone staring at them super hard. She jerked around, but no one was looking in her direction. As quickly as it had come, the feeling evaporated. What was it?

Del rubbed her hands up and down her arms to get rid of the goose bumps that had popped up. As she joined in picking up the plates and cups strewn around the lawn, she realized she could still feel power around her. Ripples of magic remained in the air, exactly like the ripples in the ocean when she threw that stone. When Del rubbed her fingertips together, a gritty residue lay between her fingers, leftover from where she had touched the brick-colored dust.

After the lawn was cleaned up and all the food that wasn't destroyed packed away, the sorcells and students trudged back toward the house. Everyone's steps were slow with exhaustion.

Eva came up beside Del. "That was wild, right?" she said. "I wonder how the wild hogs got through a protection spell."

"Yeah, wild," Del agreed.

She didn't know exactly how conjure worked, but she was sure this mess must have been her fault. Embarrassment and guilt flooded Del's chest again, filling her up. Someone could have really been hurt. She desperately wanted her shades, to pull them down over her eyes so Eva couldn't see her shame. What would Eva do if she found out Del was responsible for the spell failing? Would she tell the sorcells or Nana Rose?

"I wasn't really too worried, though," Eva continued.

"You weren't scared at all?" Del asked.

"Well, a little, sure. But the sorcells are amazing." Eva tucked her sketchbook more securely under her arm. "They had those boars caged up like—*bim!*" She lifted her hand into the air and thrust it back down like she trying to shake something sticky off her fingers. "That's the sort of witch I want to be someday. Did you see the spell Sorcell Harus cast around us? I want to know every protection spell there is. Maybe even make up some of my own."

"Did you say you want to be a *witch*?" Del asked. Were those real too? Did the school teach how to brew potions in cauldrons in the middle of the night, or cook children in ovens?

"Yeah . . ." For a few steps Eva stared at her, eyes narrowed. "Not all people who conjure call themselves witches. But some do. It's not a bad word."

Del turned away from the direction they were walking, gazing back toward the path that wound down to the ocean, the one she had walked only an hour ago. Already so much had happened. Del's head spun and she felt like she was going to fall over.

"Hey," Eva said, touching her arm. "You don't know much about conjure, do you?"

Her voice was gentle—not like the hard-edged comments other kids would make when she stumbled over her words after a teacher introduced her at a new school. When Del didn't answer right away, Eva patted her back.

"It's okay. I'm not being mean or anything. Everyone has to start at the beginning." Eva flashed her golden smile again. "Even witches."

Del took a deep breath. She still had a million questions, but first she had to sit down and think for a while.

And talk to Nana Rose. Maybe.

But Eva was smiling at her, and that, at least, was something.

"I guess that's true," Del said, tugging at one of her braids. Even if it wasn't, it made her feel a bit better.

9

As the group made their way back to the house, Del was able to get a better look at it. The building was beautiful, three floors tall, painted white with black shutters at each window. Steps led up to a porch that wrapped around the entire front of the house and disappeared off to each side. How could this be the same house she'd seen when she came in? If she had any doubts, her bags told the truth. They were right where she'd placed them earlier, in the far corner of the porch.

Nana Rose led them all up the steps to a front door made of dark, rich wood and polished to a shine. Above the door was a carving of a broom lying sideways. It was intricately detailed; Del could see the individual straws of the broom etched into the glossy wood, and even the pattern of wood grain on the handle. Underneath the broom were carvings of fat cornstalks, and a few other plants she didn't recognize.

Once everyone had climbed the stairs and were standing on the porch, the door swung inward. Waiting behind it was a man about Del's dad's age. He was tall and broad in the shoulders, dressed in an all-white suit, and there was a tight look on his dark face, as if he had a secret but wasn't about to tell it to any of them. He took them all in, and his thin mustache twitched as his eyes fell on Del. A moment later, he stood aside to let them in.

A rush of cool air hit Del, washing the heat from her skin. It felt so good, like standing in front of the freezer after she'd been outside for hours. Everyone else must have felt the same because they eagerly filed in.

"Oh, my bags," Del said, slipping through the group to grab her suitcase and backpack from the corner of the porch. Then she rushed back. Once inside, she took a deep breath of the cooled air and sighed with relief.

The house looked even larger on the inside. Giant chandeliers hung from the ceiling, making rainbow patterns of light on the walls of the entranceway. The dark wood floor was polished until Del could see her reflection. A set of carpeted stairs curled upward to a second floor, and there were so many doors and rooms that she wondered how she was ever going to find her way around.

Del turned in a slow circle, taking it all in, and that's when she saw a massive plaque above the front door. On it were two brooms, both made of honey-colored wood with tightly bound bristles to match, crossed over each other. Around them in a circle were the words "Vesey Conservatory for the Wonder Arts" in a bold, stately font. Between the two crossed brooms, another broom rose. This one had a darker wood for a handle and the bristles were woven together with cords of all different colors. A light blue ribbon lay across the bottom of the circle where all three brooms met. On the ribbon in golden, fancy letters, it read:

Protect. Educate. Survive.

The words echoed in Del's mind—they were the same ones Nana Rose had spoken earlier, the school's motto. Del remembered the story from the boat trip over, about how the people of this island had fought for their freedom, to stay safe and protected, to survive. Del turned away from the carving, a cold, sinking feeling in her stomach.

"Afternoon, Sorcell Rose. Students," the white-suited man said. His voice was deep and hollow, like he was talking from the bottom of a well. He crossed his arms at the wrists.

"Afternoon, Jube," Nana Rose replied. "As you know, we have one new addition since this morning. I'd like to introduce Del Baker." She held her palm out toward the man. "Del, this is Jube, short for Jubilee. He is the pen-pun here."

"Hello, Del. How do?" Jube's mustache twitched again, but this time it looked like his attempt at a smile. Or to hold in a laugh. She wasn't sure which.

"Hi. I'm fine." Del blinked up at the man. "What's a penpun?"

Jube's mustache twitched again. "Do you know what a butler is?"

"Yes." She'd seen lots of shows with well-dressed men who worked for rich people in fancy houses. "They do a little of everything, right? Cooking, cleaning, organizing, stuff like that?"

"I am the same." With that, he gave her a small bow.

Del wasn't sure what to do, so she decided to bow in return. Which is when she saw that Jube's feet were not on the floor, but hovering a few inches above it. Del's grip on her suitcase slipped, but her grandmother moved lightning quick and caught it before it crashed to the polished floor.

"Will you take Del's bags upstairs to her room, please?"

"Of course." He picked up the suitcase by the handle and took Del's backpack from her.

"I think we'll have her share a room with Eva," Nana Rose added. "What do you think?"

"Stellar choice, Sorcell Rose." And with that, he disappeared. Into thin air.

Del's mouth gaped open like she was a fish out of water. "H-he just . . . ," she choked out.

"I know," Nana Rose said breezily. "He's a haint. Or what you might call a ghost. They tend to do that. Don't worry, your bags will be safe."

She shook her head absently. None of the other kids milling around the foyer seemed shocked by what they'd just seen. They chatted brightly, and it was clear to Del that, like Eva, all of them had known about conjure before they'd arrived here. She looked down at her feet, feeling lost in the sea of witchy kids.

Sorcell Nyla navigated her chair down the wide hall to the base of the spiraling staircase and whispered something to Del's great-grandmother, who glanced at the gathered group, then nodded.

"Students!" Nana Rose checked a brooch pinned to her dress. "Our cookout and welcome celebration was cut a bit short, but we think it will be best to let you get acquainted with your roommates and rest up for the first day of classes tomorrow. For anyone who wasn't able to enjoy a proper supper before the incident with the boars, I'll ask Jube to deliver you each a plate—how does that sound? Now, off to your rooms, everyone!"

"No running," Sorcell Nyla called as the thundering of feet filled the foyer. She pressed a button on the wall next to a metal door and rumbling started, followed by a short chime. The door slid open and the sorcell wheeled herself in. As the door closed, she said to Nana Rose, "See you in the morning."

"This house has an elevator?" Del asked.

"Nyla is an important part of our school family. The house is quite old, but we have done what we can to accommodate." Nana Rose twirled her broom handle in her fingers. "Speaking of accommodations, will you please come with me a moment?"

Del looked over to the bottom of the stairs, where Eva appeared to be waiting for her.

"Go on, Eva. Del will join you shortly," Nana Rose said. She watched Eva jog up the stairs, then turned to her great-granddaughter. "I'm guessing you might have a few questions."

Del nodded as she fiddled with one of her braids and followed Nana Rose to the entryway of the house and out onto the porch. The sun had begun to sink lower in the sky.

"I didn't . . . I didn't know that when you said 'conjure magic,' you meant *actual* magic."

Nana Rose chuckled warmly. "Well, any old body

could see that. Now maybe you can understand why we are so concerned about preserving our history, and why we work so hard to keep what we do here a secret from all but the families who have long practiced it and our own communities out in the world. Most people assume our culture here on the island is primitive, or backward, or ignorant. Not worth knowing anything about. That's how the enchantment on the house works in fact—it shows you what you expect to see. A pretty convenient way to keep ourselves hidden, don't you think?"

Nana Rose raised her eyebrows as she asked the question, but Del dropped her head, refusing to meet her great-grandmother's gaze. A short while ago, she'd been one of those people fooled by the spell on the house. And if Del was honest with herself, she was also one of those people who had thought this island was weird and useless when she arrived. She swallowed hard. "If people knew what conjure really is, maybe they wouldn't think those things."

"If only that were true, my dear," Nana Rose said, as she paced along the front porch in front of Del. "Once, we thought sharing who we are and what we do with anyone who wanted to know might lead to greater acceptance of our people and culture. We soon realized that was a mistake."

Nana Rose's voice swirled around Del with an energy

that quivered in the air around them, like heat coming off pavement on the hottest day of the year. "People took what we taught and changed it and manipulated it and then claimed it as their own discovery, refusing to acknowledge us as the creators." Nana Rose stopped pacing and sighed heavily. "After that, we stopped sharing our ways as freely with outsiders, but the damage was already done. They had erased us from the story."

"Oh no," Del whispered.

Nana Rose leaned against the railing of the porch. She seemed worn out, exhausted. "Of course, it was no surprise when the magic they'd taken began to fade from the world. They couldn't make it survive because they didn't truly understand conjure, or respect its origins. Since then, we've worked harder to protect ourselves and our knowledge."

Del nodded in understanding. She recalled a time at her last school, when someone had taken credit for what she had done in a group science project. One of the kids in her group had presented part of what Del had researched and written. When Del told her teacher, he had said the group was getting an A anyway and she shouldn't worry about it. But Del had been really upset—she did that work herself! It wasn't right that someone else took credit for it.

"I'm sorry," she said.

"Thank you," Nana Rose said with a tired smile. "We

are still here, but we've paid a price to preserve our magic and our history. It's been a long time since this school has been full. When we were thriving, we had hundreds of students—some living here during the school year, as well as ones who would come over each day on the boats for classes, then go home in the afternoon. Now we're lucky to get twenty a year. Even our own people forget us after leaving the island. . . ." Nana Rose trailed off, and she turned away to gaze over the wide green lawn, the fields of grains, and the dense gardens.

Even though she didn't know Nana Rose all that well, the old woman's hurt brushed against Del's heart. She knew what it felt like to not have many people in your life to rely on. But . . . was Gramma one of those people Nana Rose was talking about, who left and forgot this island? Del didn't understand. How could you just forget this magic? "Did people move away and stop caring about conjure?"

Nana Rose turned back to Del. "I don't know, child. But because we keep ourselves secluded, we rely on families sending their children here each year, each generation, to learn about the culture. That isn't happening as much as it once was."

"Why not?" Del asked.

"Some hide from who we are. Perhaps they're ashamed to be the descendants of enslaved people whose families still remember. Or perhaps they feel conjure has no place in a world that is so rapidly changing."

Del didn't understand how anyone could feel that way, not after seeing all the amazing things the sorcells could do. But that's when she remembered how she herself came to be here. "Nana Rose . . . ," she began, choosing her words carefully. "Do you know why Gramma left the island?"

Nana Rose was quiet for a long time. When she finally spoke, she said, "I wish I knew, Del. But it was her choice to leave, and as much as it has pained me, I've respected that choice. As I mentioned on the boat, perhaps you and I can ask her together, when she's well."

It wasn't the answer Del was hoping for. "Well, what did Gramma say to you when she asked you if I could come to the island?"

A gust of wind ruffled Nana Rose's dress. The same wind blew Del's braids against her cheek and it felt like Gramma's kiss to wish her a good first day at school.

"When she contacted me, she was in pain. I could hear that. I hadn't spoken to her in such a long time, but she didn't have the strength to talk long. She asked if I could take care of you, that there was no one else who could. Of course I said yes."

"That was all?"

"Yes. Why?"

Shoulda told you, baby. Gramma's words in the hospital echoed in Del's mind. What was it Gramma thought she should have said? That Del had a family connection she never knew about here on Nemmine Island? Or did she mean she should have told Del about conjure? And if she hadn't told Del any of those things, what else had she never said? She thought about the memory case, the things inside that Gramma wouldn't let her see.

Even though Gramma had never said anything about where she grew up, Del never felt like Gramma was keeping any big secrets from her or anything like that. But this . . . Del shook her head. Did she even know her gramma at all? What was in that case? And why did Gramma leave all this magic behind when she left the island all those years ago? Nana Rose had said this magic was supposed to be Del's legacy. If that was true, why did she feel so out of place? It was all so confusing, and Del was desperate for answers. But they weren't ones this person she just met a few hours ago could give her.

"No reason," Del finally said.

"I suppose I'd hoped your grandmother might have—" Nana Rose stopped, waved her hand like she was brushing away a pesky fly. "Never mind. I don't think either of us should dwell on questions we can't answer. Whatever reasons your grandmother had for not telling you before, she chose to send you here now. So what do you think? Is conjure magic something you would like to learn about?"

When Nana Rose had first mentioned conjure, Del figured it would only be a few rhyming chants and some finger waggling to create some fake magic. At most she thought she'd be learning about some old traditions that didn't mean anything now. But she was beginning to understand it was so much more.

"Can I even learn conjure?" Del asked. "How do I know if I *have* magic?"

"Magic isn't something you have or don't have." Nana Rose considered her for a moment. "This will become evident as you study, but magic is something you embrace and accept in order to learn it and use it well."

Del pushed her braids out of her face. Nana Rose didn't have any reason to lie about conjure. If she was unsure about anything else, she trusted her dedication to it. "Will I really be learning actual magic, though? Like what you and the other sorcells did today?"

"Of course, along with many other things. During the regular school year, we also offer the same required classes non-magic schools teach. Our summer session, however, is all about giving students a taste of conjure, whether their families have been teaching it to them for years or whether it's their first experience. A scattering of spells, some history, broomwork—"

"Ooh! Will I get to ride a broom?"

Her grandmother froze for a moment, then her grip

on her broom tightened before she spoke again. "Maybe witches of other cultures ride brooms, but we of conjure do not. Ever. Brooms are special tools for conducting our magic. They should be treated like cherished family—with honor, reverence, and respect. Come, I'll show you."

Nana Rose led her back into the house. Along the hallway entrance, there was a line of golden hooks on the wall. Each had a vertical bar cut out of the middle. Nana Rose placed her broom into the first one, with the bristles pointing upward. She took a deep breath. "This is where the history lessons come in. Do you like history?"

"Not really."

Nana Rose chuckled as she headed toward the stairway to the rooms upstairs, beckoning Del to accompany her. "This will probably be unlike any history you've studied before."

The size of this place! The ceilings were so far above her head Del felt like a tiny speck moving through the hallways. At her previous house, she could practically touch the ceiling. Well, if she climbed on top of the refrigerator. "This house is . . . big."

Her great-grandmother opened her hands as if she were opening a book. "It has to be. This is where all students stay, as do all the sorcells. When school is in session, that is. I live here always."

"All by yourself?"

Nana Rose lifted her chin high. "During breaks, when

the students are home and the sorcells are away visiting their own families, yes. Jube is here though, and while he is not exactly living, he is good company."

"Sounds lonely."

The old woman paused on the top step. Gleeful chatter came from behind the bedroom doors on the second floor, filling the silence. But she didn't answer.

"Tell the truth and shame the devil," Del finally said.

Nana Rose smiled. "Well, at least your gramma taught you that."

The top of the staircase faced a long hallway. A long narrow strip of carpet sat atop the wood floors and ran the length of the hall. Candleholders lined the walls, which flared to life as they walked. Between each set of candleholders were framed paintings. Most of them appeared to be of various places on the island. They were so lifelike Del wanted to step into one and walk around. There was one of the house itself, another of the gardens, another of a reed-covered swampy area, and more. She was so fascinated by them she missed some of what Nana Rose was telling her.

"—and we have eight students this summer, as you know," she was saying, the bottom of her dress scraping along the carpet. "The classes are held in a separate building from this one. For now, let's get you to your room."

Del's head was swimming, filled with worry about her

gramma's health, memories of the boat ride over, the wild boar attack, the failed protection spell, and the fact that, in the morning, she'd have her first class in conjure magic.

"Here we are: room 5," she said, pointing at a small plate beside the door of a room toward the end of the hall. "If I hear anything about your grandmother, I'll let you know, otherwise I'll see you at breakfast. This is new for you, but I can tell you're resourceful and clever. I'm sure you'll handle things just fine."

With a rustle of starched fabric, she strode off and entered a door at the hall's end.

"Guess I'm gonna have to," Del whispered as she faced the door to her room.

She couldn't bring herself to go inside. Her hand rested on the doorknob, feeling the cool of the metal sink into her hand. It was so much to take in. This was her family's island, and everything here was connected to the people who had lived and died here to protect the ways of conjure magic. It was all a part of her, and yet she felt like even more of an outsider here than in any of the cities or towns she'd ever moved to in her entire life.

What had Del even more unsettled was the question she couldn't stop thinking about. The one question Nana Rose couldn't—or wouldn't—answer for her. Gramma must have had a reason for leaving this island. For never speaking to Del of this place or all the incredible things the

111

people here could do. What was that reason? The answer to that question was at the heart of why Del felt so alone in a place where her own history existed when others, like Eva, felt even more at home than she did.

And if Nana Rose didn't know what that reason was, well, Del was going to have to find out on her own.

10

When Del finally opened the door, it was to find Eva sitting at one of the two desks inside, her sketchpad open next to a long line of pencils and a metal ruler.

"Ey!" Eva said, wriggling in her chair. She faced Del and held out her arms as though she was presenting the entire room to her. "What do you think?"

The room, like everything here, was huge. Identical single beds bordered the window opposite the door, each with a nightstand next to it. Against the far right wall stood another desk and chair, a mirror image of Eva's. There was a small padded rocking chair in each corner and a wooden trunk at the foot of each bed. Even with all the furniture, the room still seemed massive.

"I took this side." Eva said. "Hope you don't mind."

How could she? Everything was the same. "No problem," Del said. "This room's so big, I could probably get on the floor and make snow angels."

"What's a snow angel?"

"It's where you lay down in the snow and move your legs and arms in and out to make an angel shape." She held her arms out to her sides and demonstrated. "You've never done that?"

"No, I've never seen snow. Except on TV," Eva said. She shivered. "Laying in the snow sounds cold."

"It is cold, but fun." Del plunked her bags on the bed.

"Oh, you can put those in the chifforobe."

"A shiff-a-what?"

Eva laughed, flashing her golden braces. "Chifforobe. It's like a closet, but instead of a separate little room, it's furniture." She pointed to a tall wooden cabinet on legs.

Del dragged her bags into the shiffa-thingy and closed the door. On the desk lay a book and a slim brochure titled *A Tour of the Wonder Arts*. Del opened it to find it was only a description of the school and the grounds. Something parents would read to decide if they wanted to send their kids here. The final page folded out into a map. Del read some of the names of the rooms: gathering room, drawing room, and the Hall of Brooms. She replaced the brochure on the desk.

114

"So what are you sketching?" she asked Eva.

"The outside of the house we're staying in. I'd started it earlier. Just putting in more details."

"Can I see?"

"Sure!" Eva patted the bed.

Del sat on the edge of Eva's bed, facing her new roommate, and the sketchbook.

"One of my favorite things to draw is old buildings. This place is double fronted—a door in the middle with windows on both sides. Windows all along the second and third floors too." Eva folded her legs up on the chair before placing the pencil on the paper again.

"Where'd you learn to do it?"

"My dad. He's an architect. When he and my mom were separated for a while—they're back together now—he would sometimes have to take me to work with him. He'd always give me graph paper to draw on." Eva placed the ruler on the page and dragged the pencil across its edge. "He showed me how to plan houses and offices and stuff. But all his work is real modern. I like older buildings; they have cool room designs filled with interesting things people don't really do anymore."

"Like rooms with no closets and two shiff-robes?"

Eva laughed. "Exactly."

Del toed her sneakers and socks off and placed her feet on the cool hardwood floor. "So your dad is an architect and your mom runs a conjure shop?"

"Yep. I wish I could do both. Architecture and conjure. Because I enjoy both. But I know it'll make Mom
super happy for me to learn conjure, so that's what I'm
focusing on first." Eva didn't look up, but kept placing the
ruler and drawing lines while sliding her bare feet in and
out of her unbuckled sandals. "What about your family?"

Del listened to Eva scratch her pencil across the paper
for a short while. She didn't know what to think about her
family, let alone what to say to Eva. She'd already told
her about losing her mom for some reason she still didn't
understand. She decided it would be best to keep everything about Nana Rose to herself for now. "My dad is in
the military. He's away on duty almost always, so I spend
most of my time with my gramma. We move around a lot."

The pencil stopped scraping along the paper. Eva lay
the pencil down and pushed her ruler to the side. Only
then did she look over at Del. "That must be hard. For
your dad to be away so much."

Del shrugged. "I'm used to it."

"So how did you end up here at Vesey?"

"My gramma went here. A long, long time ago." Del
crossed her legs and leaned her head on one hand. "She,
um, didn't really tell me all that much about it before she
sent me here. I guess she wanted me to learn all about it
from the sorcells."

"Ah, that makes sense," Eva said. She didn't ask any
more questions about her family, and Del was relieved.

"So what do you think of the place so far?"

"I don't know." Del threw herself back on the bed and looked up at the faraway ceiling. "Today I've seen some amazing, unbelievable things. Especially those brooms—I've never seen anything like them before. But it's all so different."

Eva laughed again. "Not *weird*?"

Del wanted to smile, but she couldn't manage it. "You and the other kids already know so much more than I do. And this place is so big, I feel like I'll never see all of it. And there's a ghost butler here. And—"

Eva leaned away from her desk and pressed her fingertip to Del's nose. "Boop!" she said.

Whatever Del was about to say fled her mind. "Why did you do that?"

"You were about to freak out. My mom does it too, sometimes. So my dad just boops her on the nose."

Del blinked, speechless. Eva threw her hands up. "Hey, don't look at me like that. It worked, didn't it?"

She'd never met anyone like Eva. Del laughed, and rubbed her nose. "It sure did."

"Look," Eva said, closing her sketchbook. "Sorcell Rose doesn't expect anyone to be good at everything the moment they get here. That's why it's called a school."

"Yeah, but what if I can't learn any conjure at all? What if I'm no good at it?"

Eva picked up her pencil again and tapped it against

her mouth, thinking. She seemed to really understand how Del was feeling and wanted to help. And that was something Del definitely wasn't used to.

"So what?" Eva finally said.

"Huh?"

"I said, 'So what?' to your question about whether you'll be able to learn conjure." Eva tossed her pencil on her desk and turned her whole body to face Del. "What will happen if you go to our first lessons and you aren't any good?"

Del stared at Eva for a moment, stunned by her question. "I . . . I don't know," she answered honestly.

"Do you think Sorcell Rose will stop feeding you and you'll starve?"

Was Eva serious? "No, she wouldn't do that," Del replied. She didn't know Nana Rose that well, but she was sure starvation wasn't part of studying here at Vesey.

Eva continued, "Or do you think she'll lock you in the chifforobe if you don't learn?"

Del rolled her eyes. "No, of course not. That's silly. She'd never do that."

"Then why worry? You're not here to learn all of conjure magic in one summer session. It's not even possible. Even my mom who is like . . . thirty something years old says she still learns new things about the magic all the time. She and her friends even share spells and ingredients with each other."

"She does?" Del asked, surprised.

"Sure. You don't have to practice conjure magic alone. It's a community. We help each other." Eva got up from her desk and sat on her bed across from Del. "Conjure is huge . . . and old. There's tons of stuff to learn and discover. It takes years. That's part of the reason Vesey does this summer session—so kids can find out if they like magic enough to want to spend that much time learning it. Didn't Sorcell Rose tell you that?"

Del shook her head, her braids rubbing against her cheeks. "No, she didn't. I sorta came here last minute."

"What about your gramma? She went to Vesey, right? She'd know that."

Del tugged on one of her braids while she thought about Eva's words. She'd never had a whole community to depend on before. While the idea of it was great, she didn't understand how someone who didn't even know you at all would want to help you. She didn't trust it. But she also didn't want to mess things up with the one person in this place who didn't make her feel alone. She had to tell Eva *something*.

"It's just that . . . Well, my gramma's really sick. She's in the hospital, and has to have surgery, and my dad couldn't get back from deployment. That's why I'm here."

Eva's expression changed into one of sympathy. "I'm sorry your gramma's sick," she said. "Hope she's gonna be okay."

"Me too," Del mumbled. "I guess that's why I'm so worried about doing well. I want my gramma to be proud of me, even though she didn't have time to tell me anything about this place." She didn't bother to mention that her gramma never said anything about her childhood, ever. The fact her gramma wouldn't let her look in her memory case still hurt.

"I understand." Eva stood and packed away her pencils and ruler while Del watched. "At least I've figured out what we can do before we get ready for bed," Eva said with a smile.

"What?" Del asked.

"I can tell you what I know about conjure. It's mostly my mom's stories, but they're good ones."

Del found herself relaxing around Eva, a little. She was starting to like her. If they had met in a different situation, maybe they would have had a chance to even be good friends. She put her arms behind her head and leaned back on her pillow. "I love a good story," she said.

11

Sunlight streamed through the window. Del groaned, turning over in bed. She yanked the covers up over her head to try to block out the sun, but she caught a glimpse of the clock on the table next to her bed. 6:43 a.m.

Despite the fun stories Eva had shared last night, Del hadn't slept well. She'd had another nightmare. She'd been walking the halls of a school—which of the many she'd attended in the last few years, she couldn't tell. Each class-room she passed by, the students were all looking out the door at her, staring. For a little while she could ignore it, but the staring turned to pointing. What was wrong with her? Del ran to the bathroom, breathing hard when she got to the sink. She splashed cool water on her face, then looked in the mirror. She looked the same as always. She forced herself to smile, like she always did when she was nervous at a new school—but when she did, her teeth began to fall out, one by one, clattering into the porcelain sink. Even now as the sunlight filled the room, Del shuddered.

In the bed across from her, Eva rolled over on her side and opened one eye, peering at Del. "You okay?"

"Fine," Del muttered. "It's morning."

"It sure is." Eva sat up, stretched her arms over her head. "We'd better get up. Can't be late on our first day. We've got fifteen minutes."

"What?" Del looked at the clock again, shaking off the last remnants of the nightmare. "We have an hour before class starts."

"Not fifteen minutes until class." Eva crawled out of bed and over to the chifforobe to get her bag. "Fifteen minutes until breakfast!"

"Right. Breakfast." Del wanted nothing more than to burrow back deep under the covers again. Still, even if she were home, Gramma would have already woken her up.

Gramma. Guilt hit her like a hard-thrown dodgeball. Gramma'd had surgery yesterday. Had it gone well? Was she doing okay? A sick feeling landed in Del's stomach. She needed to call her. She rolled over and grabbed her cell phone from her backpack before remembering it was useless here. If she wanted to find out about Gramma's condition, she'd have to ask Nana Rose.

"You okay?" Eva asked. Her puffy cap of coils was flat on one side and needed fluffing and there were lines on her face from the pillowcase.

Del had told Eva last night that Gramma was sick, but she didn't want to keep talking about it. They'd just met yesterday; she didn't want to be the sort of kid who blabbed their whole life to a relative stranger. "It's nothing."

Eva squinted. "I think you're what my mom calls 'scattered.'"

"What's that?" Del pulled her braids up and back, securing them into a ponytail before she too got out of bed.

Eva stuck her finger into a small jar she pulled from her bag. She rubbed the fingerful of cream in her hands and fluffed her hair. "Where you have so many things going on that you feel like parts of you are scattered around and you can't get yourself together."

Del found a bunch of school supplies—a class schedule, a notebook, some pens—in her desk, and began putting them in her backpack. "I do feel like that sometimes."

"Don't worry. I'll help you stay together." Eva picked up a towel and her outfit for the day, another matching shorts set—this one was in pale green with a print of miniature yellow pineapples. She carried it all on her outstretched hands like a huge tray. "Now let's get ready!"

Del laughed, and headed to the chifforobe to get her clothes. She'd wear shorts today too, she decided, pulling out a pair of khaki ones and a purple T-shirt.

After getting ready, the girls ran downstairs. Everyone was gathering for breakfast in the sunroom, which was kind of like a big, indoor porch. There, a variety of cereals (hot and cold) and fruit (sliced and whole) had been set up, beside bowls with yogurt, jams, honey, and more. Pitchers of water and different juices, along with teas and coffee, stood on a fancy table at the back of the room, where Nana Rose and the other sorcells were gathered, filling their cups. Del only said a quick "Good morning" to them before pouring herself a glass of orange juice.

The other students milled around, filling their own plates and cups, chattering about what the first day of class would be like. Del followed Eva to the line waiting for food. It moved quickly and she was able to fill a bowl with cereal, yogurt, and fruit. Now that she was close, she could see there was fish laid out on a plate, with some kind of thin, crispy coating. She had never heard of anyone eating fish for breakfast, but when Eva took a piece, it flaked into big chunks on her plate, and to her surprise, Del's mouth watered. She helped herself to a piece of the fish too.

They sat down at a table across from a thin, brown-skinned boy who had his plate piled up with food and was working his way through all of it. His fork and knife

124

moved in tandem, cutting and spearing each morsel into perfect bites before eating each one.

"Morning, Fino," Eva said.

Fino lifted his chin briefly to acknowledge Eva had spoken to him, but he didn't pause his eating.

"I sat with him yesterday at breakfast too," Eva said. "I think I'm going to talk to him every morning."

"He doesn't seem like a morning person," Del observed.

"That's why I'm doing it." Eva speared a grilled peach slice and bit it. "Start every day with a challenge, I say."

As Del and Eva ate, more kids came to sit with them. Eva chatted with them all while Del sat there, smiling. This was normally where she began to feel awkward on her first day at school, but Eva was so talkative and animated, Del couldn't help but feel a little bit more at ease.

Sooner than she'd expected, a bell rang, cutting through the chatter at the table.

"Five minutes, everyone!" Nana Rose clapped her hands. "Finish up, and follow Sorcell Harus to your first class." With that, she left the room. Del had hoped to catch her before class to ask about Gramma. But that would have to wait.

Sorcell Harus . . . He was the one who had looked so dusty and dirty yesterday. Del still couldn't believe he was an actual teacher. No one else, however, seemed to have any problem with his appearance—not even Nana Rose. Del supposed she had to get past it in order to learn what she needed to, especially since he was teaching her first ever magic class.

Del pushed her chair back from the table and stood. Even after yesterday, it felt unreal to be talking about magic this way. Like it was a normal part of life. Del still couldn't believe this was where her grandmother had grown up. Had Gramma ever worked magic when she was at home that she hadn't noticed—even a tiny spell? Del couldn't think of a single thing. She remembered how Gramma made her feel. Whether she was wrapping Del up in a hug, or she was waiting at home with Del's favorite snack on the counter after yet another first day of school, she was a steady presence Del could count on. Even Gramma's music stayed with her. Which was its own kind of magic, Del supposed.

But not the sort she was about to learn today.

Del took a deep breath and got up to leave for class. When she spotted Sorcell Harus, however, she almost dropped her glass.

"You all right?" Eva asked. Her tongue pushed at her cheek and Del wondered if she was trying to get a piece of food out of her braces.

"It's Sorcell Harus . . . he's . . . well . . . uh . . ." Del struggled to find the words. When she had come into the sunroom, Sorcell Harus was his usual grubby self: torn, dusty clothing; overgrown, knotty beard; ashy skin. But as Del stared, his entire form wavered, shimmered, and changed. A moment later, he looked like a totally different person. Sorcell Harus, his clothes, and his beard were neat and clean from head to toe.

She couldn't understand it. All she could do was point at him and hope Eva understood.

"Don't point," Eva whispered, gently pushing her finger down. "What about him?"

Eva must not be seeing what she was. She leaned over and whispered, "He just did a magic. Or whatever you call it. One second ago, he looked like he did yesterday: all dirty, torn clothes, hair uncombed? But now look at him!"

Eva blinked. "Um, what? You thought he looked *dirty?*"

"You didn't?"

"No," Eva said. "He always looks together. Yesterday at the cookout, he was all summery in his white T-shirt and jeans. And he's dressed up today in a white suit."

"Yeah, I mean . . ." Del waved her hand in the sorcell's direction. He was wrangling the rest of the kids who were finishing up breakfast so they could head over to the school building as one group.

"Let's go talk to him," Eva said with a decisive nod. "Maybe he can explain."

Del was embarrassed, but she didn't resist, because she really did want to know what had happened. She hated admitting she didn't know things, and longed for her phone to look up the answer. But what would she put in the

127

search box? *How do people change their appearance before your eyes?* She could imagine the results she'd get.

The sorcell smiled at their approach. "Del and Eva, good morning."

"Morning," they chorused.

"Del has a question." Eva nudged her.

Del hesitated, but Eva nudged her again in the back. When Del still didn't speak, Eva piped up.

"She wants to know why you looked like a bum to her yesterday, but not today."

"Eva!" Del gasped, horrified.

But Sorcell Harus only laughed. The sound was warm and light and unoffended. "That's an easy one to answer. Del, you may not know this yet, but we sorcells use different titles. I call myself a 'witch.' Sorcell Rose uses 'rootworker.' Sorcell Nyla likes 'conjurer.' But we all practice Southern conjure. And just like how we all use different terms, we all have our own specialties." He took a sip from his cup and placed it on the table with the emptied glasses. "You might be wondering how Sorcell Rose knew there was danger yesterday before it happened?"

Del and Eva nodded.

"We're going to discuss this in class today, but perhaps you noticed her watching the birds in the sky right before the boars burst through the trees? She is an augur, meaning she reads patterns in the world around her."

"I like how that word sounds. Aw-grrr," Eva repeated the term.

"The birds flew in a pattern?" Del asked.

"Yes. Many things in the world have or move in patterns you can read, if you know how." Sorcell Harus pressed all five of his fingertips to the middle of his chest, then touched his broom. "As for me, I am a focus. What some people call a 'looking glass,' or a mirror."

"What's that mean?" Del asked. She usually hated asking questions, but what other choice did she have? Plus, something about Sorcell Harus made her feel almost okay about admitting she didn't know something.

"Now don't be offended by this, Del, but that means each person who looks at me sees their attitude about our culture reflected back at them. If a person has positive feelings about the wonder arts, are open and willing to learn about conjure, to them I look clean, sharp, and tailored." He grasped the edges of his jacket and preened. "But if the person isn't receptive, then . . ."

"You look like a bum," Eva said.

Once again, the sorcell chuckled while Del wanted to disappear. "Yes, I imagine I must look unkempt— unwashed, uncombed; I'm not sure as I can't see through your eyes. But I can assure you, my fashion is superb."

Del bit at her fingernail. "So that means I hated the island before?"

"Not hate." He rocked back on his heels. "But it means you didn't believe there was anything worthwhile here. Now it appears you do. Which is a very good place to start."

"But . . . it doesn't bother you how other people might see you?"

He took a piece of sugarcane from the table and tucked it into his pocket. "Not at all. How a person views me is a reflection of themselves and their experiences. It has nothing to do with me. Does that answer your question?"

Eva raised her reddish-brown eyebrows and looked over at Del. Del shoved her hands into the pockets of her shorts. She understood not caring what other people think about you. It was how she managed to get through every school year since she could remember. So why did it seem so hard now?

"Yes, I think so."

Sorcell Harus gave a big, wide smile and adjusted his already perfect suit jacket. "Then let's start conjuring."

Once they arrived in Sorcell Harus's classroom, Del slid into a seat in the second row. On her left was Eva, and on her right was Joyce, a serious-looking girl with glasses. The triplets were all one row in front of her, their bald heads smooth and shiny and reflecting the morning sunlight.

Eva noticed Del fidgeting and whispered, "Don't worry. It's gonna be fun."

Del could only nod. She twined her fingers together in her lap to keep herself from playing with her braids.

"Good morning, everyone." Sorcell Harus stood at the front of the room, his back to an antique-looking blackboard. When Del looked closer, she saw the blackboard was actually a brown chalkboard, and the sorcell wrote his name on it with a piece of light blue chalk.

"This class is called Lore and Ancient Ways. That's a fancy way of saying 'history.' This summer session, we will only scratch the surface of the history of Southern conjure. Even so, I must also tell you it's impossible to know everything about what our ancestors did. Does anyone have any guesses as to why we don't know everything about where conjure came from?"

Joyce raised her hand. "Because people didn't write things down back then?"

"That is part of it. Anyone else?" When no one raised their hand, Sorcell Harus spoke again. "Another reason you might not expect is the environment. Sometimes pollution killed off plants that we would have historically used, or damaged the soil in which those plants thrived. Other times, people who weren't taking care of the land used too many of the plants and didn't allow them time to grow back, which led to some of them becoming extinct.

Whatever the cause, there are plants our ancestors would have used that are no longer around for us to use. We've had to adapt."

One of the triplets spoke up. "If we can't do things the same ways they did back then, why bother learning about them?"

"Good question, Taye," the sorcell replied. *How could he tell them apart?* Del wondered. "Three reasons. First, if you don't learn the origins of magic, you will strip away our people's influence. Our people created this magic, and we should remember that. Those who are only interested in conjure because they think it's new or fun or cool will learn only the pieces of it they like. Remember, this is an old magic born of community, and of the need to protect ourselves, educate our people, and survive in a harsh world."

"Hey, that's the motto!" said a boy on the other side of Fino, whose name she hadn't caught at breakfast.

"So it is, Jerome," Sorcell Harus said. "That is why we display it so prominently. Second: we aren't perfect. Learning ancient ways doesn't just mean learning about our ancestors' successes—it also means learning about their mistakes. Which will help you avoid repeating them. We all want to avoid that, don't we?"

Murmurs of agreement from the class, including Del.

"And third, learning your history helps you learn about yourself. There is a book in the grand house's library that lists the names of everyone who has ever attended Vesey. Some of you may come from a long line of conjurers. Ever wonder why things are done a certain way in your home? Why certain holidays are celebrated in a specific manner? Ancient ways can help you discover the reasons—and help you to preserve the magic in the event that you yourself someday need to adapt it." He snapped his fingers, alternating hands. "Plus, it will give you lots of stories to share with your family and friends. Whether they believe you or not. So: Ready to get started?"

Del and the rest of her classmates pulled their notebooks from their bags. She opened to a fresh page, pen in hand.

The next hour felt to Del like a whirlwind of information. Sorcell Harus wove lesson and story together perfectly. He talked about the reason why people throw salt over their shoulders if they spilled it. He told funny stories of a rabbit picking a fight with a statue made of tar and how to tell a bird call from a spirit call. He warned them of danger by sharing tragic stories of people getting lost in the marshes and tales of mermaids that brought storms.

"These warnings reinforce how important the marshes and the water are to our community and that we should be respectful of all they give to us: food, transportation, seclusion. Speaking of water, do you know anything about Mami Wata?"

There were murmurs around the class but no one raised their hand.

"Mami Wata is a water spirit venerated in parts of Africa and the African diaspora and is another of our connections to show the reverence we have for our oceans. Many say she looks similar to what people picture when they think of mermaids—part human, part fish. If you're lucky, Sorcell Nyla might tell you more stories about her; she's a bit of an expert." He winked at them.

Del was fascinated. And, all too soon, it was over.

"That's all the history for today."

Del glanced at the clock on the wall and was stunned to see that almost two hours had passed. Disappointed "ohhs" came from the class, and Sorcell Harus laughed. "We will have more tales for you tomorrow, I promise. But we must move on to our next lesson, and one of the most important things in our magical practice." He took the head of the cane from his belt and held it up before the class. "The broom."

Excitement bubbled up around Del, and she could feel her own heart begin to beat faster.

Sorcell Harus must have felt the energy and nodded. "Yes, you've already seen a bit of what brooms can do. In conjure, brooms hold a very special place. You may have noticed my broom, and the ones belonging to the other sorcells, are all lovingly crafted and decorated like jewelry."

Del was excited to get a closer look at the cane-shaped broom Sorcell Harus wielded. The handle was smooth, polished, dark wood. Curved lines and circles were etched into the wood and ran the entire length of the broom, all the way up to the bristles bound tightly with rows upon rows of multicolored string. In the sorcell's grip, it gave off a power Del could feel even in the second row where she sat.

"Brooms connect us to the earth, from where we draw our strength. That's why we always keep them safe, never abuse them or treat them roughly, nor do we ride them."

Shoulda told you, baby. For some reason, Gramma's words floated into her mind. Not for the first time, she wished she could be with her gramma and know if she was okay. Did the surgery go well? When was she going to be out of the hospital? She needed to find Nana Rose and ask to make a call. Like Eva had said, she was scattered. So scattered she had to force herself to focus on what Sorcell Harus was saying now.

"When we place the broom handle on grass or soil, it conducts the energy up and into bristles and provides a focus for our magic." At that, he smiled proudly.

"Any kind of conjure magic?" One of the triplets asked.

"Any kind. It's also something that ties us to this island through our ancestors. When you become skilled at wielding your broom, you will begin to feel them."

Joyce was scribbling in her notebook. She asked, "So

you can control the elements?"

Sorcell Harus shook his head. "We do not control or tame the earth's energy. We allow it to flow through as it will. That is why we must take care of the earth as it takes care of us. Any other questions?"

Del's mind whirled with so many, but she was too over-whelmed with information to form any of them.

"Okay, moving on. Does anyone know what broom bristles are made of?"

Everyone looked around, but no one raised their hand. Finally, the boy next to Fino said, "Straw?"

"Not these brooms. These are made from a specific kind of corn called sorghum, which originated in Africa. Our broom magic originated from there as well. We hold on to that connection in how we use the materials."

"Sore—gum?" Del asked, imitating the sorcell's pro-nunciation.

Sorcell Harus adjusted the silver rings on his fingers. "You got it. We cultivate it here on this island, and it's almost exactly the same, genetically, as it was centuries ago. It grows in tall stalks, much like the big-eared corn you're probably used to seeing. We use some of it for brooms, and we eat it as well."

"But what about brooms for cleaning?" Joyce asked.

"Those are completely different, and you must keep them separate. Conjuring brooms aren't for cleaning. They

136

are your companion in your magic practice." He went to the brown chalkboard and drew a picture of a broom the way Nana Rose told Del they should always be stored: handle down, bristles up. "Now, look at this picture. What does it remind you of?"

"A broom," Fino said, and the whole class laughed. Del realized it was the first time she'd heard his voice.

The sorcell gave a small chuckle. "It is a broom, yes. But what *else* does it look like?"

"A walking stick?" one of the triplets offered.

"A staff?" Eva guessed.

"Neither of you are wrong," Sorcell Harus said. "But I'm thinking of something else."

Del stared intently at the drawing. She remembered the broom her gramma used to sweep the house. It wasn't a new one, it was older, and the bristles had started to fray and spread out, almost like the limbs of—

"A tree!" Del was so excited she forgot to raise her hand; the words just flew out her mouth.

"Excellent observation, Del." Sorcell Harus took a different color chalk and drew on the outside of the broom image. "The handle represents the trunk, and the bristles represent the branches that grow up toward the sky. One of the reasons we store the brooms with the handles upright is to honor its origins, a symbol of where our magic originates."

"Sorcell Rose pounded her broom on the ground during the boar stampede," Del said.

"Knowing what you do about trees and how they feed themselves, what do you think touching a broom handle to the ground does?" Harus returned his cane to its rightful place, hooking it onto his belt by the loop in the carved bird's neck. When no one spoke, he touched the blue chalk image of the broom and the yellow chalk image of the tree drawn around it. "What's missing?"

Del bit her lip. Branches, trunk . . .

"Roots," Del said.

"They pull water and nutrients from the soil," Eva added.

Harus pointed at them both. "Great job working it out. Bringing the broom handle in contact with the earth helps in charging it, bringing energy up the trunk into the branches or bristles."

"Is that why it's also known as 'rootwork'?" Eva asked. "Because it's working to make a connection between us and the earth?"

"Good, Eva. That's one reason, yes. I'm glad you're all making these connections and beginning to understand the origins of Southern conjure, and why the broom is so important."

A bell rang, signaling the end of the class and bringing more unhappy groans that the lesson was over. Del didn't think she'd ever been in a class where she wanted to stay longer and learn more.

Sorcell Harus smiled. "Don't worry, class. I'll have more stories for you tomorrow. Lots more. Right now, you're about to take part in a special ceremony. Follow me to the gym."

12

As Del and her classmates followed Sorcell Harus through the hall, outside, and across the deep green grass toward the gym, she felt a warm glow wrap itself around her. Maybe she still didn't know much about conjure, but she was learning how it fit into the world she did know. This magic from a people—her people—who were brought to this country: afraid, trapped, without freedom, who tried to create a little bit of peace and safety in their lives.

Protect. Educate. Survive.

The same way Del made the connection between the

broom symbolizing a tree, she made another connection. Even though Nana Rose knew Del could have had no information on conjure, she still allowed her to come here to the island for the summer when Gramma contacted her.

Del swallowed hard.

Nana Rose took a chance in allowing Del to come to Nemmine Island. There was no way she could have predicted how Del would react to learning magic was real. And when she refused to do the protection spell yesterday, the resulting stampede showed Nana Rose had been right about how dangerous it was to let people in who didn't take magic seriously. Del had endangered the school even more than it already was, and put the survival of her people's magic in jeopardy.

Gramma . . . why didn't you ever tell me? She felt sick to her stomach. Gramma trusted her to do so much: help pack before each move, navigate in the car, even to remind her when she needed to take her medicine. Gramma didn't trust her with this family knowledge and that stung. Maybe if she knew what had happened on this island to make her not want to pass along the magic or share any of the items in her memory case, Del could figure out if there was a place for her in the world of conjure magic.

Del was trudging along the crisp grass behind the other kids toward the large building that must have housed the gym when she froze in her tracks. There it was again.

That feeling she'd had at the cookout. Like someone was nearby watching her. A crackling on the surface of her skin.

Eva had continued on for a few steps before she realized Del was no longer with her. "Come on, slowpoke. I think I know what's going to happen in the gym, and we don't wanna miss it."

Del nodded, but as she was about to take a step forward, she saw something out of the corner of her eye. Movement, to her left. Maybe coming from behind one of the smaller buildings lining the path from the classroom to the gym. She whirled around to see—

Nothing there.

Del frowned. She was sure someone was lurking around—she could feel it. "Did you see that?" she asked Eva.

"See what?" Eva squinted under the bright sunlight and glanced around.

"It was something dark and blurry." Del pointed. "Over there."

"Dark and blurry? Like a shadow?"

"Maybe. It moved when I tried to look at it."

Eve shrugged. "Whatever it was is gone now. Could it have been a bird, or the wind moving tree branches?"

Del had been so sure someone was watching her. But with each passing moment, it felt more and more like Eva was probably right. She shook her head. "You're probably right."

They hurried across the rest of the lawn and finally arrived at the gym doors just as the rest of the class was lining up. Sorcell Harus pushed open the double doors and let the kids filter in. It looked like any other gym that Del had been in. A large, open space, with polished wood floors, high ceilings, and lots of sports equipment scattered around: jump ropes, balls of different sizes and shapes, padding for elbows and knees, and helmets. Across another wall was a set of bleachers, and in front of them were Nana Rose and Sorcell Nyla. The women were next to a table covered with a heavy woven cloth.

"Come in, everyone," Nana Rose called.

The students filed in eagerly. Except for Del, who approached more cautiously.

"Since this is your first official day of class, we wanted to familiarize you with an essential item for conjure magic practitioners." Nana Rose's voice projected throughout the space, making Del's ears ring.

Sorcell Nyla spoke next. "This is an item that is a hallmark of conjure, as you've just learned. It is a part of your wonder arts journey, and it will stay with you for a lifetime in some form or another. We are giving these to you as gifts, and we hope, with time, they will become companions."

Del's eyes widened. She leaned forward on her toes and shoved her hands in her pockets to try to calm herself.

"These brooms were made especially for you attendees of this summer session, but if you decide not to continue with the wonder arts, we ask that you return them in the best possible condition. Do we have your agreement on that?" Sorcell Nyla asked.

Cheers of "yes!" went up from the gathered students and this time, Del's voice was among them. She glanced over at Eva, who was trembling with excitement and bouncing on the balls of her feet.

Sorcell Nyla went over to the left side of the table and faced the crowd, then whipped off the cloth like a magician revealing a trick. A row of brooms lay on the table, all of them different. The wooden handles varied in colors from beige to chocolate brown. The bristles were all various shades as well, some with multiple colors on the same broom.

Nyla gestured to the table. "After you choose a broom, we will begin our lessons in broom etiquette, so all of you will know how to handle, store, and care for your broom."

Sorcell Harus joined the other sorcells. "The broom you receive today may not be the one you use forever." He took his cane broom from his belt and spun it between his fingers. "Once you graduate from Vesey, you can choose another, one that suits your individual personality. You may add charms, braid, crystals, or other elements that will change its appearance or help you carry implements to aid in your journey to protect, educate, and survive. One day, you may even craft your own broom."

"So come up here, one at a time, now," Sorcell Nyla said.

Each student went up to the front of the gym and selected a broom. Fino's toast-brown bristles were woven together with red cord, and Joyce's was a bright yellow with orange cord. Each of the triplets chose a different shade of blue with black braiding. The broom Eva returned with was almost as tall as she was; the braided cord holding the rainbow-colored bristles was salmon pink.

Del was last, and by the time she reached the table, there was only one broom left: a red-bristled broom bound with green-and-yellow cord. She reached out to pick it up by the pale wooden handle, and the moment her fingers closed around it, a flash of energy rocketed up her arm, and she saw the briefest flash, a vision of a room, painted in pale green. She yelped in surprise.

Her eyes shot up to ask the sorcells if she'd done something wrong, and that's when she saw a dark shape hovering behind Nana Rose, flickering.

It was the same shadowy shape she thought she'd seen earlier. But in the time it took her to blink, it was gone. In the warm gymnasium, Del's body went cold. Nana Rose rushed forward, placed her hands on Del's shoulders. "Are you all right? What happened?"

Del still gripped the broom handle in her fist, clutching it for all she was worth. Nana Rose loosened Del's fingers. "Don't choke it," she whispered.

"It's okay," Del finally said, trying her best shake off both the vision of the room and the shadowy figure. "I'm fine."

Nana Rose nodded, and Del took her place by the other kids. What was happening to her? None of the other kids had reacted strangely to getting their brooms. She took slow, deep breaths, hoping no one had noticed.

"Broom etiquette is Sorcell Rose's department and we yield the floor to her now," Sorcell Nyla said.

Nana Rose began by asking everyone to repeat a spell blessing the brooms. Del was sure to repeat it this time, word for word, along with the rest of the students.

"I will now go through proper handling." Nana Rose raised her broom, the polished dark wood and shells catching the afternoon light. "Bristles facing up is the correct holding and carrying position. You must also store it with the bristles facing up, as Sorcell Harus told you earlier."

One of the triplets raised their hand. "Sorcell Harus said touching the earth with the handle draws magic up into the bristles. Is that why we need to store them upright?"

Another triplet asked, "Or is it because keeping the bristles up helps it hold on to magic? Like keeping a lucky horseshoe turned with the open end up?"

"No," Nana Rose said with a smile, affectionately running her palm over the head of her broom. "It's so the bristles don't get crushed."

Everyone laughed.

"Just a little joke, everyone. All of your reasons are valid." Then Nana Rose gave them a quick introduction to several aspects of broom use: how energy is drawn up from the earth, how to twirl the broom for air spells, and how to use the broom to focus magic. As Del watched, an ache started in her heart. It felt so *right*. Even though she was new to all this, she could feel the strength coursing through Nana Rose's broom, and she couldn't wait to try the movements out for herself.

But when the sorcells had the students spread out and try some broomwork on their own, Del's broom didn't seem quite so eager. She followed all the basic instructions Nana Rose had given them for drawing energy into the broom, and yet—nothing. She tried replicating the demonstrated movements, but the broom didn't feel any different from the cleaning broom at home.

Eva wasn't having the same trouble with her broom. Her roommate was able to get the hang of the two-hand movement used for overhead twirling, and the rhythm for pounding the earth to call up energy. Del couldn't. But she felt the power pulsing next to her as Eva's movements became smoother.

147

Del tried again. Her broom handle grew warm, then cool. It twisted . . . and then, suddenly, tried to pull away. Del had to hold tight to keep it from leaving her behind. She picked up on a strange vibe, and she recognized the feeling—it was the same feeling she usually got from kids when she started a new school. Did the broom . . . not like her?

As quickly as it tried to tug away, the broom stopped trying to flee her grasp. In fact, all the energy she'd felt from it a moment ago was gone. Remembering Nana Rose's warning, she loosened her grip, not wanting to choke her broom.

Del's breath came in gasps; the effort of holding on to the broom had winded her. Gently, she stroked the bristles. "I'm sorry I grabbed you so hard before. I didn't know," she whispered. The broom was still, and tears pricked the corners of her eyes.

She'd broken the protection on the island by not participating in the spell, and now she might have strangled her brand-new broom so hard that it didn't have any interest in her. All in her first twenty-four hours on the island. That had to be a record. For this magic to be a part of her family's history, Del certainly wasn't doing well.

"Isn't this the coolest thing ever?" Eva was breathless, her eyes bright as she joined Del.

"Yeah, it is," Del mumbled. She could feel her roommate's broom vibrating with energy. Del's, however, remained quiet and still in her hands.

"What's up?" Eva asked when she noticed Del's expression. "Something wrong with your broom?"

"Nope! Everything's fine."

Her words were light, but her insides were churning. Del didn't want to be the only one with a faulty broom. Or a broom that had taken an instant dislike to her. What if Del didn't have a strong connection to magic at all? It was possible that she'd grown up too far away, or maybe too much time had passed for her to ever be good at conjure. Maybe the broom knew that. And if the broom wouldn't cooperate with her, it wouldn't be long before everyone else knew it too.

If Eva started to believe she couldn't work conjure, what would she think? And Nana Rose had been so sure Del would be able to learn conjure; if she found out Del's broom wasn't accepting her, would she decide Del shouldn't bother with classes anymore?

Maybe Gramma left the island because she wasn't able to control a broom or work conjure as well as Nana Rose expected her to. Maybe she was scared of the expectation being Nana Rose's daughter placed on her. Was it possible that Gramma left because she was feeling the same things Del was feeling now? Lost and alone and a little overwhelmed?

Del told herself over and over that she was capable,

just like her dad said. She was going to handle it, like she always did. No one needed to know about her or the broom. Soon, she started to calm down, like she had cast her own magic spell.

In order to figure this all out, she needed to know more. Fortunately, she had a lead: the book Sorcell Harus had mentioned. The one that listed every student who had ever attended Vesey. He had said it was in the library. So that's where Del would start.

"Don't worry." Eva's hand landed on Del's shoulder. Del nearly jumped; she'd forgotten Eva was still standing next to her. "Remember, we can practice together!"

"Thanks," Del said. And despite all the things battling inside her, she really meant it. "I'll meet you back at the room, okay? I want to ask Sorcell Rose something."

As everyone filed out of the gym for lunch followed by independent study time in their rooms, Del made her way over to her great-grandmother, who was already approaching her.

"Nana—I mean, Sorcell Rose? I wanted to ask if you heard anything about Gramma." Del tucked her broom firmly under her arm and stuck her hands in the back pockets of her shorts. "I'm worried."

"I was going to speak with you about that." Nana Rose placed her hand on Del's shoulder gently. "I received some very good news earlier today."

150

"What is it?" Del held her breath.

Nana Rose smiled wide. "Your gramma's surgery went perfectly. She's in recovery, and will be at the hospital for a little while, under observation. But according to your father, it appears she will be absolutely fine."

The news was exactly what Del needed to hear. In fact, she was so excited, she hugged her great-grandmother tight. When Nana Rose returned the hug, Del realized what she was doing. Embarrassed at her impulsive actions, Del let go and stepped back.

"Sorry," she muttered. "I don't know why I did that."

"It's okay, Del. It brought me a great deal of comfort and happiness." Her smile was warm, but Del pulled her gaze away to focus on the door to the gym. "Is there anything else you wanted to talk about?"

Briefly, Del considered asking Nana Rose about the vision she'd had when she picked up her broom for the first time—the one about the pale green room. What did they call that color? Seafoam green? Also, she wondered if she should mention the shadowy form she'd been seeing around the house and grounds. Nana Rose must have known about visions, or haints, or whatever it could be— she had probably even seen something similar in her many years of running this school.

But what if she didn't? What if she thought there was something wrong with Del, or that these things all meant she couldn't learn conjure anymore?

"No, thanks," Del said. "I just wanted to make sure Gramma was getting better."

Before Nana Rose could reply, Del rushed out the gym to catch up with Eva. She could use all the studying time she could get.

13

That night, Del lay in bed, waiting until Eva was fast asleep. Once she heard her roommate's slow, even breathing, she pulled back her covers and got up. When Eva had been in the bathroom, Del had gotten into bed still wearing her clothes, so all she had to do was wedge her feet into her sneakers.

She only hesitated for a moment on her way out before grabbing her broom. Even though it was still unresponsive, part of Nana Rose's broom etiquette was making it feel like a companion. Del couldn't do that if she left it behind. She made sure to carry it with the bristles pointing upright, but when she tried to walk through the door, the broom spun her hand horizontally, and the handle banged into the doorway. Stifling her gasp of surprise, Del grabbed the broom handle with her other hand to stop it from clattering again in the quiet night.

"Shh!" she whispered. "I'm trying to be sneaky."

Whether the broom was listening or not, it didn't try to mess with her again. Once she was through the doorway, she paused. She heard Eva's soft snuffle, indicating she hadn't woken up, and Del released the breath she'd been holding. Then she closed the door softly behind her.

Del looked to the right, at the end of the hallway where Nana Rose's rooms were. Straight across was the room two triplets shared, and to the left were Fino and Jerome's room and the room Joyce shared with the third triplet. Nothing moved. All she had to do was creep past a few doors, and then it was all empty rooms between her and the stairs.

Thankfully, the dense carpet absorbed the sound of her steps. She made it to the staircase and held on to the banister as she tiptoed to the bottom. Past the elevator and around the corner she crept, then through the sitting room and living room. The entire house was dark, except for the shafts of moonlight that penetrated the curtains and left patterns on the polished wood floor. The stillness of the house, so strange after the rumbling excitement of kids during the day, weighed on Del. She looked around as she stepped forward, making sure to stay in the patches of light. There were so many shadows now: on the walls, in the corners. . . . Was the shadow she'd been seeing around the island among them? Del's heart raced at the thought and she rushed to get out of the dark and to her destination.

Finally, she made it into the room marked on her student brochure as the library, and she slipped inside, closing the door softly behind her. The room was comfortably cool, and well-lit by the moonlight streaming through the windows and the fireplace that sprung to life as she closed the door. It was a little smaller than she expected, though still much larger than any room in any house she'd ever lived in. Bookshelves lined three of the four walls—the wall with the fireplace was bare except for one of those lifelike paintings she'd seen in the upstairs hallway above the mantelpiece. Two large, comfy-looking chairs faced the fire, each with a footrest.

Del stared at row after row of books. Most of them had no writing at all on the spines. How was she going to find the book Sorcell Harus talked about? Was she going to have to look through every single one? That could take all night. Maybe even all week.

She took a deep breath in through her nose. Dust particles flooded in and she quickly covered her nose and mouth as she sneezed. It wouldn't be good if she got caught in here. But who would be up at this time of night? She thought about Jube. He was a ghost—did they have to sleep? She held her breath until she thought she might explode, but she didn't hear anything, so she finally returned to her mission.

Something Eva said to her earlier about how even witches needed to start at the beginning echoed in her memory. Del lay her broom across one of the chairs and took as many books as she could carry from the bottom shelf to the left of the door and brought them back over to the fireplace. She dumped the books on one footrest, plunked herself down, and began flipping through pages.

Skimming the text in each one quickly made it clear that none of them were about the school's history or previous class lists. She did see several interesting spells, though. There was the Hot Foot and the Pebble Bed, names that made her chuckle. Then there was the Calling, which looked like a communication spell. It looked really complicated; it could only be performed in the Hall of Brooms, which Del remembered hearing about in the brochure, and required a group of people to perform, kinda like the protection spell.

To find the information she needed, though, she couldn't just read about spells all night. Instead, she picked up each book and shook it, thinking maybe something would fall out. When it didn't, she fanned through pages. Nothing.

She brushed her braids out of her face and leaned back in the chair, craning her neck to look up at the rows and rows of books that went up to the ceiling. This was going to take forever.

She groaned at the thought of picking up and carrying the heavy hardback volumes back and forth from the shelves to the footrest. "Ugh, I'm already done with this."

To her shock, the books flew up into the air. Del leaped to her feet, then ducked as one by one, they shot over to the bookshelf and nestled back into the spaces she had plucked them from. Did she do that?

Cautiously, she said, "Can I have the next book on that shelf, please?"

No books shifted or lifted from the shelves. No magic. She collapsed down into the chair again. It would take her the whole month to go through all these books.

"If only this place worked like my phone," she whispered. "I could just search."

What are you searching for?

The voice came from all around Del, from each of the four walls. It wasn't one she recognized either—not Nana Rose's, not Jube's, or any of the sorcells'. She looked all around but there was no one here. She was alone. Did Nana Rose have some kind of voice tech installed? If so, it wasn't like any she'd heard. She crept around the room, but saw no devices anywhere. Confused, she sat back down and stared at her broom in the matching chair next to her.

"Broom, what is going on? Any ideas on how to find the book?"

157

She didn't expect it to respond, and it didn't. But the voice did, again.

What are you searching for?

Del flinched. Did she have to be sitting in the chair to activate it, whatever it was? She stayed in her seat this time, holding on to the padded arms while she spoke.

"I heard there is a book in here that lists the names of all of the students who ever attended Vesey Conservatory."

Accurate.

Del folded her arms. "Um, can I see it?"

A thick volume wedged itself out of the top corner of a bookshelf opposite the fireplace and hovered in the air above Del. *Student Roster*—compiled by Robert Vesey, she read on the spine. Was he a relative of hers? That would be cool, to get to meet more family. She reached up, and the book moved away.

Del looked over at her broom and it was shaking on the chair next to her.

"Oh, so that's funny?" *Great*, she thought. *It won't help me do any spells, but it will laugh at me.* She addressed the voice again. "May I please hold the book?"

The book drifted down to lay on the footstool in front of Del.

"Thank you," she said, opening the cover. Some of the pages were fragile with age. Rather than flip through the book's delicate pages, she tried something else. "Search for Violet June Vesey."

158

Violet June Vesey, born Violet June King. Page 473.

"Thanks." Del hadn't even thought of searching by her grandmother's birth name instead of her married name. Good thing she didn't have to. She turned to the right page and there it was: both of her gramma's names alongside dates of when she was a student, the classes she took, her grades in various courses. The book also included all kinds of other stuff as well, things that were way more interesting. There were notes about her being in the school choir, which wasn't surprising, since Gramma was an amazing singer. What did surprise Del was that Gramma was an excellent swimmer and a basket weaver— Del had never seen Gramma swim or weave any kind of basket. Her project had won second place at the county's science fair when she was fourteen. There was even a list of academic awards she had won:

Candle dresser of the year, age 10

Watergazing champion, age 12

Best broomworker, age 14

Hex throwing finalist, age 15

One thing was clear: Gramma had been an excellent conjurer. That was one theory down. Del hadn't *hoped* Gramma had been bad at magic, but at least it would have been an answer as to why she left, and maybe even the reason Del's broom wasn't working for her like everyone else's. She looked over at her broom now, but it was quiet, making her feel even more alone, if that was possible.

She went to read the rest of the entry—but there was nothing. Well, there was a list of classes and grades, and a note of Gramma's graduation, when she was eighteen. But there were no more interesting bits about clubs and friends and awards. Something must have happened between when she was fifteen and when she finished school and left the island. "Are there any other books that include student records?"

No, the volume you hold is the only one.

Del fingered the edge of the page, and was about to turn it down to mark her spot when a sniff sounded in the room. *Books in this library are not to be damaged or defaced in any way, including dog-earing. Please utilize a bookmark.*

"Um . . . sorry. Is there any other information anywhere on Violet June Vesey?"

Ten by ten, books of all sizes lifted off the shelves and hovered in the air. Covers opened. Pages flicked by. Bookmarks lifted. Sooner than Del expected, the books returned to their shelves.

"Maybe there are some books in other rooms?"

Searches include all accessible rooms on school grounds.

"You can do all that from here? Won't that wake up people in the house?"

I am the librarian. An offended huff of air. *Of course I can and no, it won't.*

Nothing else, anywhere in the house, about her gramma. As far as she could tell, all Gramma did between when she was fifteen and when she left the island was go to class—no clubs, no awards, nothing. Del leaned back in the chair and exhaled. What changed when Gramma was fifteen? Was it the same thing that made her want to leave home and never speak of it again?

Lines from a song Del knew by heart drifted through her mind.

I ain't spending not another day
Living this way

"Not Another Day." The song Gramma recorded when she was young—not long, it seemed, after she left Nemmine Island. A song about lost love. Did she fall in love with someone at school? Did she have her heart broken, and that's why she didn't want to spend another day here?

The clock on the wall let out a gentle chime. One in the morning. It was getting so late—or early, depending on how you looked at it. While she was disappointed she didn't turn up any helpful information, it felt good to discover more about her gramma's past. In a way, it felt like they were growing closer, even when she was still miles away. But she should get back to bed before anyone found her here.

"Thank you for your help," Del said, climbing out of the chair. "If you come across any other information on why my gramma left this island, do you think you might let me know?"

The librarian let out a gasp. It bounced around the room, coming from everywhere at once. *You are Violet Vesey's granddaughter? Sorcell Rose's great-granddaughter? Why didn't you say?*

Del closed her eyes and groaned. How could she accidentally reveal herself to an invisible librarian? "Um, yeah. But I'd really like to keep that a secret."

Don't fret. I keep many secrets. But you did not answer my question.

Something about talking to an invisible librarian made admitting this easier for Del. She didn't have to look into anyone's eyes and see pity or concern. "Well, I didn't even know about my great-grandmother or this place until a few days ago. Before that, my family was me, my gramma, and my dad. I wasn't really looking for a bunch of family history when I came here."

Hmm. And yet . . . here you are. Searching . . .

"That's not— No. I'm curious, that's all. And I want to know why my gramma left. But since there's no information on that in any of these books, I'm out of luck."

Not all information is in books. Speak to Lundy, maybe he can help you.

"Lundy?" Del had completely forgotten about the giant gator who'd brought her here. Only after everything else she'd seen here could a gator the size of a school bus slip her mind.

She didn't want to seem ignorant or disrespectful but

she had to ask. "How can I? I don't speak alligator."

Then it's a good thing he understands English.

"Of course he does," she muttered, picking up her broom. "Thanks for all your help."

Good luck, little legacy.

Del left the library as the flames in the fireplace winked out behind her, leaving only moonlight to guide her steps.

14

Del quietly hurried down the dimly lit hallway, headed back to her room. In the darkened house, shadows lingered everywhere and she had no idea if one of them was the shadow she kept seeing from the corners of her eyes. Nervous, she hummed a few bars of Gramma's song to calm herself down. Thankfully, the staircase didn't creak, like the stairs in some of the houses she'd lived in.

Light leaked out from under Nana Rose's door at the end of the hall. She could see shadows move in that thin strip of illumination, like someone was pacing on the other side. Hushed whispers flooded out as she got closer, and before she knew what she was doing, Del was bypassing the door to her own room to listen at her great-grandmother's.

She kneeled, her broom in one hand, its handle against the floor. The door was one of those old-fashioned ones with a big hole where the key should go, like the doors in the old black-and-white movies she watched with Gramma on Sunday afternoons. She peered through the keyhole, catching a glimpse of Nana Rose's yellow dress. This close to the opening in the door, it was easier to hear who was speaking.

"So we have no idea why the protection spell failed?" Jube's tone was calm and even.

"We don't," Nana Rose said. She crossed the room, and Del could now see a narrow table with spherical candles in column-shaped candleholders and a jar containing feathers on the surface. "Perhaps one of the children's minds wandered, and the boar stampede was simply a coincidence. In any case, Nyla, Harus, and I have seen to it. The protection will hold for the rest of the summer session."

"My question was not about the boars," Jube replied. He drifted into the center of the room where Del could now see him. Instead of his white morning suit, he now wore a black one. Apparently, ghosts could change clothes. "I was wondering if anything else could have slipped through when the barrier was weakened."

At his words, Del froze. That shadowy presence she'd been seeing throughout the school. Could that thing be what Jube was talking about? Her refusal to participate might be even more serious than she knew. Her head spun with the possibility she let in an evil presence. *No one else can even see the shadow except me. I don't even know if it's real.*

"My concern is not imagined threats slipping through the barriers," Nana Rose grumbled, "but the very real threats on our doorstep. We only have eight students this summer session—the fewest in Vesey history. I have no idea how much longer we can stay open, but the children, no matter how few, need this knowledge."

Jube stood still, his hands clasped behind his back, as Nana Rose began pacing again. Silence for a few of Del's speedy heartbeats. Then he said, "What will become of us?"

Someone stepped in front of the keyhole, blocking Del's vision. "Remember our motto." Nana Rose's voice had changed. It lost the desperate edge that it'd had a moment before; it was gentle now, comforting. *"Protect. Educate. Survive.* Because we always make a way when there is none." With that, her voice dropped lower. "Even if there are only eight new students."

"Seven," Jube said, "were it not for Violet calling, and Ms. Delphinia Baker arriving."

Del shifted again, so she wouldn't miss what they were saying. But her legs were numb and wouldn't hold her weight. She wobbled, making the floor beneath her creak in protest. Del froze in place as the brush of Nana Rose's skirts scraped the door.

"Ah, yes, Del." Her great-grandmother moved over to a chair and sat down. "She shows much promise, but she is so closed off. To us, I think, and to herself."

"Who can blame her?" Jube said in response. "Violet obviously never spoke of the island. Nor why she left. Have you talked to her about her grandmother?"

Del held her breath.

"I have no idea why Violet felt she had to leave. You know that," she replied, and Del exhaled. "She had finished school and she was legally an adult. It was her choice to make. I'd never been able to stop her from doing anything once her mind was made up."

"I'm aware," Jube said. "There was only ever one person who could."

"And by that time Bobby was gone." She adjusted her skirt, smoothing the fabric with her palms. "Del's only been here two days and she's been awash in things she's likely struggling to accept, much less understand. Not just conjure, but myself as well. We only have a short while together and at the end of that time, I don't want her to be as angry with me as her grandmother must be."

Del leaned so close to the door that she slipped, her broom clattering to the floor beside her.

"What was that?" Jube asked.

He was fading, about to reappear in the hall to check out the noise, Del guessed. She scooped up her broom, shot to her feet, and without looking back, sped down the hall, wrenched open the door to her room, and threw herself inside. Then she spun around, closed the door behind her and leaned against it, panting.

Was Nana Rose going to come to her room? Was Jube? It's possible she'd made it back to her room before Nana Rose could open the door but how long did it take a ghost to disappear and rematerialize? If they did know she was eavesdropping, what would either of them say? Could she get in trouble? Did magic school have detention?

Del waited for a little while longer, but no one came to her door. Everything was okay. She stood up and walked toward her bed. She should probably get under the covers and pretend to be asleep, just in case it was taking Nana Rose a while to figure out what had happened. She still needed to be quiet though; she didn't want to wake Eva up. She was probably—

Oh no.

Her lamp was on, but Eva wasn't in bed. Last night she had the covers pulled up over her head, leaving only her reddish-brown puff of hair visible. Now the covers were thrown aside, her roommate nowhere in sight. Had she noticed Del wasn't in her bed? She should have piled up some pillows under the covers before she left to make it look like she was. She vowed to do that tomorrow night, when she was going to sneak out and find Lundy to—

"What're you doing?"

"Ahhh!" Del yelped and shoved her broom forward like a weapon to protect herself. When she saw it was Eva, she nearly collapsed in relief.

Eva stepped out from behind her open chifforobe door and pushed Del's entwined fingers aside, moving the broom. "That's not exactly the form Sorcell Rose showed us at the demonstration today."

"You scared me!"

"I didn't mean to. I was getting a quick snack from my suitcase." She held up a bag of roasted sunflower seeds. "What were *you* doing?"

Del clutched her broom to her chest and rocked back on her heels. "I . . . uh . . ." She couldn't think up a story fast enough, and if she stalled any longer, Eva would know she was lying anyway. "I snuck down to the library. I wanted to check out that book Sorcell Harus mentioned so I could see if my grandmother really went here."

Eva nodded as she tore off a corner of the bag to pour some seeds into her palm. "Did you find out?"

"No. I mean, yes."

Eva gave Del a skeptical look, then popped a sunflower seed in the shell into her mouth.

"I mean . . . I found the book, and she was a student

here. But I wanted to find out why my gramma never mentioned the school before." Del could feel herself looking around the room, trying to figure out what to say. Hopefully Eva didn't notice her scrambling for words.

Eva took the shell from her mouth, now sucked clean of salt, and lightly bit it. It cracked open and she ate the tiny seed inside. "Sounds like something you'd have to ask your gramma, not find in a book."

That was *exactly* what she wanted to do right now, more than anything. Jube said there was only one person who could ever change Gramma's mind once it was made up. But Nana Rose said that person, Bobby, was gone. Gone where? Was Bobby the Robert who compiled the book? Maybe they were related. She had to find out who that was, and where he went. "I can't exactly do that right now."

"Why not? Is your gramma that sick?"

Del counted the loops of cord holding the bristles of her broom together. "Um, Sorcell Rose said that the only working phone on the island is in her office, and, well . . . I don't exactly want to ask my gramma about it with her listening in."

Eva rolled up the bag of sunflower seeds and secured it with a rubber band. "Then I've got some good news for you about tomorrow's conjure lesson." She headed over to her desk and flipped pages in their primer, yawning as she handed it to Del.

As Eva crawled under back into bed and pulled the covers up over her head, Del looked down at the page she'd flipped to. It read:

Watergazing.

15

Del stayed up another hour studying the watergazing chapter. She didn't nod off until well past two in the morning, and ended up sleeping through her alarm. Eva did as well, and by the time both girls dragged themselves out of bed, washed, dressed, and stumbled downstairs, everyone had already eaten breakfast and was leaving the sunroom.

Eva didn't seem to mind that Del's late-night antics had kept her up, but she was grouchy about missing breakfast. "Look, there's Jube. Let's go see if there's any food left."

"Good morning, girls," Jube called. "I was about to clear the tables, but I've saved you some fruit-filled pancakes. You can eat them on the way to class." He handed Del and Eva each a buckwheat pancake wrapped around fresh fruit with a drizzle of honey. He'd tucked them into pieces of crisp paper so they could eat them on the walk to the school building.

"Thanks, Jube!" Del said.

"You're the best!" Eva added.

"We might have embarrassed him," Del said, after he smiled gently and faded into mist.

"Come on, let's go!" Eva took off through the front door and across the lawn, munching on her pancake wrap. Even though Del was taller, she had to rush to keep up with her roommate.

"I read the chapter last night," Del said around a slice of apricot. "Sorry if I kept you up."

"That's okay. I'm a little tired, is all."

"This is you tired? Whew," Del said, panting with the effort of keeping up with Eva's long, bouncy stride.

Eva laughed. "Hopefully it'll all click for you in class today."

They finished their quick breakfast and tossed the paper in the trash can outside Sorcell Nyla's classroom, then pushed open the door. The other students were already seated in chairs that formed a circle. In the middle of the circle was a small table.

"Come in, girls. We're just starting," Sorcell Nyla said. Today, a blue-and-green blanket covered her legs, picking up the colors in her headwrap. She gestured to the only seats left, the bracelets on her left wrist jangling softly.

"Thanks," both girls mumbled as they took seats next to each other. Fino sat on the other side of Del. On Eva's other side sat Kaye—Del only knew because today her name was written on her shirt in big sequined letters.

Sorcell Nyla clasped her hands together and her bracelets collided with a bright jingle. "Students, today, I'm going to teach you about a very special practice called watergazing. Who knows what that is?"

Del had read the chapter, but she still hoped the sorcell wouldn't call on her. Thankfully, Joyce raised her hand.

"It's a way to look for things that might be lost." Joyce pushed her glasses up.

"It is. What else?"

"Seeing the future," Taye and Faye said at the same time.

"That too. We'll get more into sight work when and if you decide to pursue higher levels of conjure education." Sorcell Nyla moved her chair around the outside of the circle. "Today we're going to focus on another use of watergazing. How many of you would like to speak to a family member or friend back home?"

Del perked up. This was what she was waiting for—it was exactly what she'd read about in their textbook last night. She'd thought they were going to listen to a lecture today, but if they were going to actually try watergazing . . . she might be able to talk to Gramma.

Sorcell Nyla pushed the sleeves of her blouse up her arms. "On this table is a clear bowl of water. You—"

"Is it tap water?" Kaye asked.

"Could be bottled water," Joyce said.

Faye opened her mouth to reply, but Sorcell Nyla cut her off. "Girls, please. It's rainwater. I placed a grain or two of sugar in there as well."

The hair on the back of Del's neck stood up. She remembered the other night, in Gramma's hospital room— there had been a bowl filled with water on the table by her bed. Could that have been how she'd contacted Nana Rose? In the book from the library Gramma was listed as a champion watergazer when she was studying at Vesey.

And what had the librarian called Del? *Little legacy.* Maybe she would be able to do this.

Del was eager to raise her hand. "What is the sugar for?"

"Good question. We use sugar if we think the conversation will be difficult and we want to sweeten the person we're trying to talk to."

Del glanced over at Eva and found her roommate rubbing her hands together in anticipation.

"Who are you going to contact?" Del whispered.

With a fierce look on her face, Eva said, "My cousin.

175

She never returned my box of colored pencils. I'm gonna tell her they better be back on my bed when I get home. How about you?"

"My gramma."

Eva nodded. "I figured."

They returned their attention to the demonstration. Sorcell Nyla moved to the outside of the circle. "One at a time, you will all come up and give it a try. Focus your eyes on the bowl. Don't look at the water, look *through* it. Think of who you want to contact. Think of their voice, their image, and what message you want to send. And once you have that focus, try to hold it. Who's first?"

Del bit her lip. *Look through the bowl.* What did that mean? The bowl was clear and so was the water. But she wasn't going to have to go first, because Fino was already strutting over to the table. He sat down and leaned over the bowl, his nose almost touching the water, his eyes open wide so it looked like he was trying desperately not to fall asleep.

"Relax," Sorcell Nyla said. "Breathe. And it's okay to blink."

Fino stopped staring so hard, but even from where Del sat she could see his breath rippling the water in the bowl. Everyone was quiet.

And that's how they sat, for a full minute. Right as Del was starting to squirm in her seat, Fino's lips moved. She couldn't hear what he was saying, so she learned forward to listen.

Eva tugged her back. "Nosy," she whispered.

Finally, Fino laughed. "All done," he said.

"Good job." Sorcell Nyla pressed her palms together.

"What happened?" Del asked.

Fino looked uncomfortable, and Sorcell Nyla spoke up. "It's perfectly fine if anyone would like to keep their watergazing conversations private. Now, who's next?"

The triplets all rose at once and sat in a semicircle around the bowl. They seemed to have no issue contacting whoever it was they tried. Joyce went next, and was soon grinning and whispering. Soon it was Eva's turn, who hunched over the bowl, watching it closely. After a few moments, she nodded solemnly with a little frown on her face, like she was listening to some important instructions she didn't want to follow.

Sorcell Nyla finally gestured to Del. "Last but not least."

She slowly got to her feet and crossed to the center of the circle. Everyone's eyes were on her. She reached the table, pulled the chair out. It released a high squeak and the other kids snickered.

Del sat and stared into the clear bowl, not knowing what to expect. She tried to gaze through the water, as Sorcell Nyla instructed, but after what felt like a long time, she had seen and heard nothing.

Try again. Gramma could do this. So can you.

She looked through the water at the tiny bubbles

clinging to sides of the bowl. Every so often, a bubble would loosen from the side and float to the top of the water, and break when it reached the surface.

Gramma, she called out in her mind. *Are you there? Are you okay?* She thought the words in the same annoying voice she sometimes used, the one that irritated her gramma so much, hoping that might provoke a response. The water sat there in the bowl, undisturbed, while Del's eyes began to dry out from staring so long.

Her head was starting to hurt and her eyes were itchy. She reached up to rub at them, and it felt like her arm was moving in slow motion, as if she was trying to punch through soft clay. What was going on? As her hand headed toward her eyes, it crossed over the bowl of water. That was when the whole room went blurry.

Everything around Del fuzzed out—everything except for the bowl of water. It was crystal clear. The voice that appeared in her head sounded like someone shouting from across a giant canyon.

Del?

Gramma? Is that you?

Ok— said the voice.

What did you say? Del called. *Oak? Are you saying you're okay?*

"Oak," said the voice again. "Oak."

What do you mean, Gramma? Are you better from your surgery? Are they taking good care of you?

Del thought the questions as hard as she could, but she could already feel the connection loosening, the room around her growing clearer, the conversation with Gramma unraveling until it was gone.

She gasped for breath, and felt Sorcell Nyla's hand on her back. "Easy, Del. I think that's enough for your first watergazing session."

Del coughed, then locked eyes with her teacher. She wanted to tell Sorcell Nyla she wasn't finished, that she had to try again because she was only beginning to get the hang of it. But a wave of exhaustion came over her, and she just nodded.

As she moved back to her seat in the circle, though, she smiled. She had done it. She'd worked conjure. She'd talked to her gramma, and knew she was okay. *Everyone has to start somewhere. Even witches.*

"That's it, everyone!" Sorcell Nyla called, clapping her hands and sending her bracelets singing. "I'd like you to read more on watergazing on page fourteen of the *History of African American Magic* in your room. Now, though, you might consider taking a walk outside. Communing with nature is a key part of your conjuring journey. In an hour, we'll break for lunch and then we'll resume afternoon classes."

Everyone began gathering up their things, chatting excitedly as they got up to leave. Del, however, decided to take her time.

"Are you okay?" Eva waited for her at the door to the classroom.

"Yeah," she said, glancing over at the other kids. She bit her lip. "Can we talk? Upstairs?"

Eva nodded. As the other kids proceeded outside into the sun and heat, Del and Eva made their way across the lawn to the grand house. When they got back to their room, Eva plopped down on her bed.

"So, you gonna tell me?"

"Tell you what?"

"What really happened." Eva unbuckled her sandals and they tumbled to the floor one at a time. "You had a strange look on your face when you finished."

Del sat down on her bed. She wasn't sure how much she should share with Eva. But she had to talk to someone.

"I tried to contact my gramma, and I did. I asked her if she was okay."

"What did she say?"

"That's the weird part. It sounded like she said, 'I am oak.'"

"Are you sure she didn't say 'okay'?" Eva sat back and swung her legs.

"That's what I thought. But she said it twice, exactly like that. 'Oak.'"

"It could have been a funky connection. Maybe because your gramma is far away? Or because she's sick?"

"Maybe . . ." She hummed to calm herself.

"You hum or sing that tune a lot. What is it?"

Del tugged at one of her braids. "It's one of my gramma's songs."

"Songs?"

"Yeah. My gramma was a singer for a long time. She recorded a song in the seventies called 'Not Another Day.' They still play it on the radio sometimes."

"Cool!" Eva said. "I think I recognize the tune, maybe . . ."

At that moment, Del bolted upright. *Gramma's song.* Didn't it say something about an oak tree? She ran through part of one of the verses again in her head:

I stand under my oak tree
And wonder why you can't see
That I'm barely holding on

And so I'm leaving
On that bus this evening
Why can't you ask me to stay?

Was Gramma trying to tell her something about the island? Something about why she'd left? Del had to talk to her again. She thought for a moment, then grabbed the book from her bag and opened it to the section she'd read last night.

Watergazing involves looking deeply into water of a specific

181

quantity and source, as a way to focus your energy to find answers to questions, contact others, and glimpse the future. See also: divination.

She showed the words to Eva. "Remember how Joyce and the triplets were debating what sort of water was in the bowl?"

"Yeah."

"Well, this passage makes it sound like the source of water has an effect on the conjure. And that the *quantity* of water does as well."

Eva rolled over on her back, her head hanging off the side. Del mirrored it, laying on her back on her own bed.

"You're thinking you need more water."

"Exactly." If she could increase the amount of water she was using, maybe she could make a stronger connection between her and Gramma.

"But how large of a bowl could you use?" Eva asked. "Maybe we can ask Jube for the biggest bowl in the kitchen?"

Suddenly, Del flipped over on her front. *The ocean.* That was the most water anywhere. The librarian told her to speak to Ol' Lundy anyway—maybe tonight she could find Lundy, and try gazing into the ocean as well.

"What?" Eva asked.

"Um . . . I . . ." Del had almost forgotten for a moment that Eva was there. "Nothing. I thought I had an idea, but I don't think it would work."

Eva narrowed her eyes. "You're going to sneak out again, aren't you?"

"No, I just . . ." Del avoided Eva's questioning gaze as long as she could, but her roommate didn't look away.

Eva put her heels on the edge of the bed and circled her knees with her arms. "Then what is it?"

Del couldn't tell Eva her plan. If she did, she knew Eva would insist on coming with her, and that couldn't happen. She wanted to ask all the questions that had been plaguing her since she arrived, but now she had new questions to ask. Did Gramma know why her broom wouldn't listen to her? Did she have any idea of what the shadowy thing was, and if it was Del's fault it was here? She had a hundred questions—and Eva couldn't know about any of them, or she'd know Del had lied to her, and had maybe even put the entire island at risk. There's no way she'd live that down.

Del scratched her head. The scarf she used as a headband to tie her braids back slipped and she tugged it forward. She could talk her way out of this. "I was thinking . . . that I could go down to the ocean. But then I realized that's a silly idea."

"No, it's a good idea." Eva tapped her finger against her bottom lip. "The shore isn't terribly far, but it wouldn't be easy to walk there, especially in the middle of the night."

"Exactly. So that's why—wait, what?"

Eva raised her eyebrows. "Well, if you don't want

anyone noticing what you're doing—as I can tell you don't—
you probably thought you'd have to go after hours." She
smirked. "And I already know you're willing to sneak out."

"Yeah, I guess you do." Del couldn't help but smile.
"You're right about trying to get to the shore at night,
though. Bad idea. I'll have to come up with something
else."

"Maybe not." Eva spun around and picked up the
school's brochure. She flipped through the glossy pages
until she got to the map. "The ocean might not work, but
how about a swimming pool?"

Del eyed the image. She had to admit, it was an even
better idea than trying to watergaze in the ocean. Quieter,
easier to get to. Now she needed to figure out how to
shake Eva.

"That's a really good idea! But you don't have to come
with me. I . . . um, don't want you to get in trouble."

"Uh huh. I've been in trouble before so it's cool." She
got up and gathered her shoes from the floor. "I want to
help."

"But . . . why?"

Eva buckled her sandals. "Because we're roommates.
Because I have a gramma too and I don't get to see her a
lot and I know how it feels to miss her. Because if you're
going to try to sneak into the school pool in the middle
of the night, you're going to need someone watching your

back. But mostly because I'm a nice person, duh."

"Eva—" She flopped back on her bed, and groaned. This girl did not know how to take no for an answer.

The more Del thought about it, maybe it wasn't so bad that Eva wanted to come along. She could be the lookout to make sure none of the sorcells caught them. And at the watergazing lesson today, most of the kids were able to talk to the person they're contacting without anyone else hearing them. Del could make sure Eva wouldn't be able to hear her while she spoke.

She looked at the alarm clock on her nightstand and got up to put her socks back on. "How does midnight sound?"

"Great!" Eva said. "Spell for the perfect summer: *Learn some magic, make a friend, connect with family once again.*"

Breeze blew through the window; refreshingly cool on the burning embarrassment heating her face. Did Eva really think of her as a friend? Already? Del's secrecy about who she was and what she was planning to do ate away at her. The thought of what Eva might say if she found out . . . All Del could do was try to keep her secrets as close as possible and solve the mystery as quickly as she could. At least the summer session was only a few weeks. Shorter even than the time she spent at any other school she'd been in, and she got through those just fine.

As she wedged her feet into her sneakers without untying them, a bell clanged, signaling it was time for lunch. Eva rushed to the window and peered at the line of kids making their way back toward the school. "Let's go! After that on-the-run breakfast, I'm starving!"

Del followed Eva out their shared room and closed the door behind her.

16

The alarm went off at one minute past midnight. Del had set it to the lowest volume so it wouldn't wake anyone but her and Eva. As she pressed the button to stop the buzzing, she looked over at her roommate. Eva was already awake. Del had been too, but that was because she couldn't fall asleep.

Del pushed off the covers, then shoved her feet into her sneakers. Eva got up as well and buckled on her sandals.

"Ready?" Eva asked, grabbing her broom. "Oh, and here." She held out her hand; in it were a few packets of sugar. "I snagged them at dinner. Just in case," she said with a shrug.

"Thank you," Del said. She hadn't even thought about the trick Sorcell Nyla had told them earlier. But Eva had. She was a considerate person and Del felt a tiny bit bad that she had invited her along only to be a lookout. Del shoved the packets in her pocket and tucked her broom under her arm.

The girls crept out their room and jogged down the darkened hallway. There was a strange sound Del hadn't remembered hearing the night before—something like *tap, tap, click, sweep.* She tried to figure out where it was coming from, but it kept getting farther and farther away. It wasn't a broom sound. It paused, then started again.

Tap, tap, click, sweep.

"What is that?"

"No idea," Eva replied. "Keep going."

As they continued down the hallway, they noticed a lamp was still lit. Del was glad someone had accidentally left it on; it was much easier to move around the house than it had been last night when she visited the library.

They made it to the end of the corridor where circular staircase led down to the first floor where another lamp emitted a soft glow. Was Jube still up and around? They would have to be really quiet. Eva led Del down a narrow pathway that wrapped around the back of the building. Del hadn't been down this way before.

"It was part of the tour," Eva whispered. "Before you got here."

Del could smell the water. Lights embedded into the walls and floor around the pool burned steadily from behind a layer of thick plastic, pushing back the dark. With each step, she could almost hear the water calling to her. In the back of her mind, a tiny feeling skittered across her shoulders like a bug.

Something was wrong. It was the same feeling, one of being watched, that she'd had since she arrived. For a moment, she thought of turning back, making some sort of excuse not to continue. But she didn't know what excuse Eva would believe. So she ignored that skittering feeling and pressed on.

She and Eva continued following the scent of water down the hallway. Her sneakers made a small squeaking sound on the tiled floor. They arrived at a set of double doors, pushed one of them open, and slid inside.

The pool was lit from the under the water by small lights attached all around its bottom edges and the slight movement of the water cast rippling patterns on the walls and ceiling. The entire room shimmered. Del thought this must be what it was like to be inside a diamond, looking out. An occasional lap of water hit the side of the concrete pool. While being near the ocean or lying down in the bathtub was usually a relaxing experience for Del, right now she felt on edge.

Del walked around the pool to look out the window onto the grounds. Eva joined her. There was the call of a bird outside, likely an owl gathering its family to hunt. The Vesey Conservatory looked so different at night. She wondered if Ol' Lundy was out there and if she could find him in the darkness. Maybe it would be better to look during the day, when she had a better chance of finding him without accidentally stepping on him and getting eaten.

"I guess we'd better get started, huh?"

"Yep." She and Eva kneeled down at the shallow end of the pool opposite the diving board, making sure to keep their brooms away from the edge.

"Are you gonna get in?" Eva asked.

"I don't think so. The pool is like a giant bowl, right? Hopefully, I can look in from the edge and get enough focus built up to contact Gramma."

That strange feeling came over her again. She shook it off, and turned to Eva, who was regarding her with wide eyes. "You'll be lookout, right? Make sure no one gets in here?"

"Yeah, of course." Eva spun on her bottom to face the door to the pool. "Go on whenever you're ready."

"Maybe you could go stand by the door? So you can hear if anyone is coming?" Del didn't want to make Eva suspicious again, but she didn't want her nearby to overhear. She held out her broom to Eva.

Eva hesitated for only a moment before nodding. She took Del's broom and her own over to the door.

Del shivered, and shook her head to clear it. All she

needed to do was get to watergazing so she could talk to Gramma. She leaned forward to look into the water and saw the bottom clearly. Sorcell Nyla's instructions were: Don't look at the water. Look *through* it.

"Come on," she whispered to herself. "You can do this."

A full minute went by. Nothing. Sighing in frustration, Del got up and walked down to the deepest end of the pool to try again. She leaned forward, one of her braids slipping free of the scarf she used to tie her hair. After tucking it behind her ear, she repositioned herself, and took a deep breath in through her nose, preparing herself to look deep.

That's when she heard it again. *Tap, tap, click, sweep.*

It wasn't close, but it was closer than it had been when she'd heard it before. Could it be one of the sorcells, still awake? Those few lamps had still been lit, but she'd thought it was an accident. It was possible someone was still up, walking the halls.

Only, it didn't sound like any sort of walking Del could imagine.

Don't worry. There's no danger. The sorcells recast the protection spell. But Jube's words nibbled at the edges of her mind. Could something have really gotten onto the island while the barrier was weakened? And suppose, just suppose, it's been waiting . . .

Stop.

If Eva were beside her, she would have booped Del's

nose. Del shook her head and gave a small laugh. The sound reverberated in the large room, off the concrete and the still water, and Eva turned and gave her a confused look. Del just shrugged.

All right. Enough of that. Focus. Del stared into the water from where she kneeled at the edge of the pool. As she did, something began to form in the water.

No, not in the water. That was a reflection. The thing taking shape was behind her. Del froze, wide-eyed and unable to move as the dark shadow gathered itself into the shape of a person. A person behind her, looking over her shoulder. In one swift motion, Del shot to her feet and spun around.

There was no one there.

But she had turned too quickly, and her feet slid from under her. Time slowed as Del began to topple backward. She felt weightless as panic flooded her insides while she tried to regain her balance, but it was no use.

With a shriek and a splash, Del sank into the surprisingly warm water, headed straight for the concrete bottom, as if something was pulling her there. Even in her shock, she knew it would be *very bad* if her head hit the rough concrete, so she twisted in the water, thrashing her legs to stop her plummet to the pool's depths. Through the water, she thought she could hear Eva shout her name, the soles of her sandals slapping against the concrete as she ran to the edge of the pool. Her face appeared above the water, and she was shouting something Del couldn't make out.

Del was a decent swimmer, but she never got in the water without covering her hair. Even though she managed to keep her head from pounding against the bottom, the rough surface of the pool floor caught the coils of her hair. Del pushed against it, pulling her braids off the bottom of the pool, but the long tendrils of her hair floated free—and as she shot up toward the surface, they were tugged into the filtration system.

The filter was like fingers, twirling into her hair and holding her fast. She thrashed, but she couldn't get her face to the surface of the water. Her legs floated upward, and with her hair caught, Del turned upside down in the water. She kicked harder, faster, but she wasn't able to get her hair untangled. She tried to reach behind her and disentangle her hair from whatever was still holding her, but she couldn't feel anything. Why couldn't she get free?

Something touched her face, her hair. She wanted to scream, but she knew she couldn't. All that would do was let water in. She fought against the touch with both hands, kicked her feet.

There was a big splash, and a second later, Eva's face appeared near hers. Her short cap of hair wasn't in danger of getting caught. She motioned to Del that she was going to untangle her hair. Under the water, Del nodded. She could feel Eva tugging, and as a few braids loosened, she was able to lift her mouth above the waterline and take a breath.

Tap, tap, click, sweep.

It was the sound again. Fear raced up her spine.

Eva fingers worked faster. They spun over her hair like little spider legs. What was she doing? It didn't matter. As long as she got free.

Tap, tap, click, sweeeep.

It was getting closer.

"Can you hear—?" she tried to ask Eva, but water splashed in her mouth and she spluttered.

"Almost got it!" Eva said. Or at least Del thought that was what she said; her ears were still submerged. She tried to lift herself up again only to be yanked back.

The sound was closer and faster. Like it was rushing toward her. Whatever the thing was, it was coming toward them. Eva wasn't paying attention, and Del couldn't turn her head enough to see it. The bottom of the pool vibrated with the approaching sound. Del braced to punch whatever it was in the nose. Or kick it in the stomach. Whatever she could reach.

Finally, Eva's hands slid away and Del's hair came completely free of the vent. Del made to lift herself upright, but as she did, a powerful grip enclosed her arm and wrenched Del up and out of the water. Gasping for breath, Del looked toward what had grabbed her.

She was face-to-face with Sorcell Nyla.

"Del! Del, are you okay? Say something!" Her voice was distant and Del turned her head to let water drain out of one ear. That's when she noticed that Eva was caught with a similar grip in the sorcell's other hand.

Del coughed, feeling miserable. "I'm okay. I think."

"Eva?"

"I'm fine too."

Del pushed her soaking wet braids out of her face and found Eva had had to undo several of them in order to get her free. That's when she realized Sorcell Nyla couldn't have been in the pool in her wheelchair. She cast her eyes around the room, and sure enough, Sorcell Nyla's chair was off in a corner.

"You're walking!" Del managed to say.

"Yes," the sorcell responded. "Did you think I couldn't?"

She moved around the edge of the pool, leading the girls along. *Tap, tap, click, sweep.* "I'm able to walk for limited periods. Not everyone who uses a wheelchair needs to use it all the time. Sometimes it's only when their legs need support."

Del was struck speechless when she looked down. Not because Sorcell Nyla was using her legs. But because she didn't have any.

Well, technically she *did* have legs—they just weren't human ones. And there were six of them. Four of them were long and thin, bent in the middle, and came to a point at the tip. The other two were just as long, but they each ended in a flat, round flipper, almost like the oar on a rowboat.

"But you have . . . too many legs," Del whispered.

This time Nyla laughed as she set the girls on the edge of the pool. "I've never heard it put that way. But you're wrong. This is in fact the correct number of legs for me. I am part human, part crab. Blue swimmer crab, to be specific."

"But how can—" Del stopped. "I've never heard of a part human, part crab!"

"Just because it isn't your experience, doesn't make my experience untrue," Sorcell Nyla replied, flexing her many-jointed legs. "Many of the stories Sorcell Harus has told you in his lore classes were examples of connections between us, the Caribbean islands, and the African continent, no? Do you remember his tale of the sea goddess Mami Wata? Here in this part of the world, we call her Mammy Watah, and she has many daughters. I am one of them."

"Okay . . . ," Del said, embarrassed. "Sorry for asking. And for staring. That was rude."

"I appreciate that my appearance may be surprising to you, but it *is* rude to stare. Thanks for apologizing." Sorcell Nyla descended into the pool, moving smooth as a dancer. She wore her hair tied up out of sight, and her swimsuit was a shimmering blue color that almost matched the blue-brown color of her multiple legs. She checked the filter before returning to the girls. "Now, shall we talk about why I found you and Eva in the pool after midnight, fully clothed, when I'm about to go for my nightly swim?"

Del and Eva exchanged glances. Del wiped the water out of her face, squeezed the ends of her braids.

"I . . . ," Del began. She didn't want to lie, but there was no way she was going to tell the sorcell or Eva she saw something—someone—in the reflection of the pool, making her slip and fall. And she didn't want to have to explain about Gramma to yet another person.

Sorcell Nyla's gaze sharpened. "You came here to watergaze."

Eva piped up. "It was my idea. Del's connection wasn't great in class, and so I suggested we might try here."

Del was shocked silent. She had no idea why Eva was taking the blame when she didn't have to. She glanced over to see what her roommate was thinking, but Eva wasn't looking at her.

The sorcell pressed her lips together for a moment. "I see." She pushed herself up out of the pool by her arms, her bracelets clattering against the pool edge. Her crab legs came out of the water one at a time, and tapped to the surface. The flippers swept the ground as she stood. "Are you homesick?" she asked.

Del decided she could tell a bit of the truth without

inviting too many questions. "My gramma is in the hospital. I wanted to make sure she was okay."

Sorcell Nyla returned to her chair and motioned for the girls to follow her out of the pool room. "I understand. I think we should all maybe have a chat with Sorcell Rose." She looked over her shoulder at Del and Eva. "First thing in the morning, that is."

Del and Eva sloshed over to retrieve their brooms before following Sorcell Nyla to the elevator. They rode up in silence and when the doors dinged open, Del and Eva trudged out. A moment later they were back at the door to their room.

Sorcell Nyla patted each girl on the shoulder. "Go get changed into some dry pajamas, you two," she said. "Then get some rest. Sorcell Rose will want to see you first thing in the morning."

Eva fumbled with the doorknob, her wet hands sliding over the metal. Del helped her turn it and they both tumbled inside. After they closed the door and set their brooms bristles up in their racks, Eva let out a nervous laugh. "Well, we're both in trouble now."

"You didn't have to say it was your idea," Del said.

"I know, but it saves you from taking all the blame. It's what friends do, duh."

Eva went into their bathroom and got a towel for each of them. Wrapped in the soft, sweet-smelling towel, Del peeked out at Eva.

"Thanks for being there. If you weren't I might have—"

"But I was there, so don't even say it."

Del didn't say it, but she thought it. She was grateful to Eva for saving her and for taking the blame for the idea of using the pool to watergaze in the first place. She shivered when she thought of what could have happened to her if she had been alone in that pool. How would Nana Rose have felt then?

After shuffling over to her bed like a zombie, Del sat down. Her hands went to her hair and rebraided what Eva had to loosen to get her free of the filter system in the pool. And what about Gramma? How would she have felt losing a daughter *and* a granddaughter? This was terrible. Dad was so right: she would never have been able to take care of anyone. Why did she think she could?

Eva got changed, then sat down across from Del on her own bed. "Why did you fall in the pool?"

Del blinked. "I slipped."

"Really?" Eva said. "Because before you fell, I saw you stand up quick and look behind you, like you saw or heard something. Was it . . . was it the same thing you thought you saw in the hallway yesterday?"

Yes. "It was just . . . It was nothing."

Eva didn't look away. "You can tell me, you know. Is there something going on with you?"

A million things. But they were her problems, not Eva's. Her roommate was already going to get in trouble for trying to help. And whatever that shadow person was . . . what if it tried to hurt Eva because she was around the next time it decided to come after Del?

Eva didn't need to get tangled up in all of Del's business. Del would handle it, the same way she always did.

"Nothing's going on with me. I'm just worried about my gramma, that's all." Del spread another dry towel on top of her pillowcase.

Eva stared at her for such a long time Del had to turn away. But a moment later, all she said was "Hey, I've got something that will cheer you up."

She headed over to the chifforobe and pulled out a woven tote bag almost as big as she was. After digging around in it for a few moments, Eva held up a tiny packet. She grabbed a pen from her desk and sat next to Del with the package. It was a brand-new pack of chewing gum.

Eva pulled the strip from around the top to open the pack and expose the five sticks of gum inside. "Here, take one."

Del pulled one stick from the pack. As soon as she did, though, Eva snatched it from her.

"Hey!" Del said.

"Hold your horses a minute. This is one of the first spells my mom taught me. I've never used it before, but this seems like a good time."

Carefully, Eva unwrapped the foil so the inner paper showed. She wrote Del's name and her name next to each other on the paper and just as carefully folded the stick of gum back up. She closed her eyes and whispered a few words. Then, holding the stick of gum with the thumb and first finger of each hand, she tore it in two. One of the halves she handed to Del.

"If I did it right, you should have my name and I should have yours."

Del peeked at her half. "You did it right."

"Cool!"

"Now what?" Del asked.

"Now you chew your gum," Eva said, popping her half into her mouth. "It's supposed to make sure we stick together as friends."

"Cool," Del said, laughing as she chewed her piece. Fruity sweetness flowed over her tongue.

This was the first time in ever that someone had wanted to keep her as a friend, much less done a spell to make it so. It was a possibly the most special thing someone other than her family had ever done for her.

I made a mistake letting Eva come along tonight, she thought as Eva smiled at her. *She could have gotten hurt. I won't let it happen again.*

17

Turned out Nana Rose was pretty mad in the morning.

"I am so disappointed with both of you girls." Her usual crisp, pleasant voice was gone and she spoke in tight, sharp tones as she paced back and forth in her office, her arms folded. "You both know better than to be in any pool area without supervision. I cannot believe this! What in the world made you take leave of your good sense?"

Del stared at her feet in shame, but even as she did, she was stunned at how much Nana Rose sounded like Gramma. Gramma rarely got angry, but like Nana Rose, she would say she was *disappointed*—and that, for Del, was much worse.

"We were only—" Eva began.

Nana Rose cut her off. "Sorcell Nyla informed me of what you thought you were doing. I expect better of you, Eva. You're from a conjure family. You should know to ask for help with something like watergazing, instead of just trying things all willy-nilly."

"Yes, Sorcell Rose." Eva hung her head.

"I will have to inform your mother of this." Nana Rose turned to Del. "Please excuse us. Eva and I have a call to make. But don't go far. You and I will be speaking next."

Del looked at Eva, whose eyes were wide. Del shuffled out Nana Rose's office and stopped when she heard the door close firmly behind her.

Del felt awful as she slunk back to their room. What was Nana Rose going to say to Eva's mom? How much trouble was Eva in? Del had always thought the worst thing was having to rely on someone else to help you with your problems. Turned out another person taking the blame for something you'd done was even worse.

Del glanced at the alarm clock on the bedside table. Everyone would be in class with Sorcell Harus right now. That's probably where Del should go until Nana Rose called for her. But . . .

Del bit her lip. There was something she needed to do

203

without Eva knowing and this would be the perfect time. She needed to talk Ol' Lundy. Going now would mean she wouldn't have to explore the overgrown parts of the island at night. And besides, there was no telling how long Eva would be in Nana Rose's office or what Nana Rose would do to Del when she was done with Eva. She might confine Del to her room for the rest of the month, maybe even create some sort of barrier around the house that only worked on Del.

If she was going to find out what Ol' Lundy knew, this might be her only chance.

Del grabbed her broom and headed for the door. She jogged down the hall and down the stairs, turned the corner, and headed toward the front door. That's when she saw Sorcell Nyla seated next to one of the bay windows with a book on her lap.

She pressed her back against the edge of the hallway to hide. Sorcell Nyla didn't react, didn't look up. Del let out a breath. What could she do now? There was no way to walk to the front door without passing too close to the teacher. Del now knew she was part human, part sea creature—who knew what kind of special detection powers that gave her? Del couldn't risk it.

The back door, maybe? But that was through the kitchen, and Del still had no idea when and how Jube would appear. Yesterday, he'd risen up through the floor at lunch to refill her drink and Del nearly jumped out her skin in surprise. If Jube saw her leaving, Nana Rose would be the next person he'd tell . . . for sure. She couldn't risk that.

How do I get outside?

She remembered the brochure for the school. There was a map in it; maybe it could tell her if there were any other exits. But it was upstairs in her room, and she didn't want to chance going back to get it. She spun the broom around and around in her hands, then let the handle of the broom slide through her fingers until it touched the floor. She tapped it softly against the wooden floorboards, trying to come up with an answer. It was hopeless. She leaned back against the wall, eyes closed, and blew one of her braids out of her face.

That's when she felt someone tugging at the broom.

"Huh?" Del's eyes popped open. There was no one there. Sorcell Nyla was still around the corner. Who was—?

The next pull was harder, like a dog tugging at a leash. It pulled Del away from her slouch against the wall, and she almost toppled over. Quickly, she regained her balance.

"It's you!" Del whispered to her broom.

Her broom hesitated only a moment before taking off, yanking Del along with it. Her feet slid across the polished floorboards, Del barely able to hold on as it maneuvered her through hall after hall, down a precariously steep staircase, and whipped her around several corners, until they reached a narrow door. Del had to grab the edge of the doorframe to stop her momentum.

"That," Del huffed as she caught her breath, "might be the best ride I've ever been on! Better than any roller coaster."

The broom said nothing, just tugged her hand gently toward the latch. Before opening it, Del looked to the left and the right. The coast was clear, so she eased open the door and slipped inside.

This was a room she'd never been in before. In fact, she'd never seen a room like this at all. It was like a garage, but for boats. The boat she'd come to the island in was here; she'd recognize it anywhere. She wondered if Ol' Lundy had carried it in here once she and Nana Rose left the beach. Now that she looked closer, she could see the name on its side: *The Flower Girls*. Nana's name was Rose and Gramma's was Violet. That couldn't be a coincidence.

Along the walls, there were fishing rods, nets, and wooden boxes, as well as oars and life jackets. Even though there was no air-conditioning in here, the room still felt cool and comfortable. Another door ahead of her led outside. Del pushed it open and walked through.

"So this leads down the path to the marsh," Del said to her broom. She recalled seeing the marsh on the map, but didn't pay much attention to it, except to notice how large it was. Sorcell Harus had told then in class how important the marshes were to their ancestors and to the local ecosystem and its wildlife today. Many of them had escaped enslavement by hiding in the marshes and eventually establishing whole communities there. How they managed to do that, Del had no idea.

What she did know was that alligators were cold-blooded, and liked warm, sunny spots to lie in. The marsh had plenty of areas without trees and full sunlight. Maybe that was where Lundy would be, soaking up as much heat as possible. It was as likely a theory as any.

Del followed the well-trampled path toward the marsh. Her broom was quiet in her hands; she supposed it was okay with her taking the lead now. Maybe it was finally starting to like her. The sun was out, and Del turned her head up to face it. Her skin was cool from having been in the air-conditioning since yesterday afternoon—and going to bed with wet braids hadn't helped. She let the sun's rays chase the last of the chill remaining in her body while she walked.

An angry hiss stopped Del in her tracks. She looked all around her.

"Uh-oh," she whispered.

Del had been so wrapped up in her own thoughts that she hadn't been looking where she was going. But she was about stumble right onto an alligator.

It wasn't Ol' Lundy. This creature was smaller, but no less terrifying. The gator whipped its head back and forth, then hissed again, showing its craggy teeth. Del flinched backward, her wits enough about her to make sure she wasn't going to step on anything alive. That's when she glanced around her, and she froze.

She was standing on a raised mound of hard-packed dirt, overlooking the marsh. She was also standing in the middle of a congregation of alligators. Their scaly bodies nearly blended into the various colors of the reeds and grasses surrounding the marsh, but as she watched, they slowly turned to face her, gazes sharp. They were all sizes, from small ones no longer than her leg to massive ones that were almost as big as Ol' Lundy.

And none of them were happy she had invaded their favorite sunny spot. There were threatening growls and more hisses. In fact, they looked ready to chomp down on her. Del was too terrified to move. But her broom was not. It wrenched itself free of her grip and flew off toward the marsh, leaving her alone to deal with the territorial reptiles.

"Hey!" Del shouted after it. "Where are you going?"

But there was no answer. It had vanished into the tall grasses.

"Figures," Del muttered. But she didn't have time to dwell on her broom abandoning her. The gators' eyes were all locked on her, following her every movement.

She stepped back once more then held her hands up in a gesture of surrender. "I'm sorry. I wasn't paying attention to where I was going."

One of the gators, a big one, snapped its jaws and headed toward her. Del shrieked and tumbled backward, falling hard on her bottom.

"I didn't mean to! I just wanted to speak to Lundy. That's all!" She used her hands and feet to crab walk backward away from the reptiles. She moved as fast as she could on her palms and heels, but the gators, even with their short legs, moved *fast*. "I just wanted to ask him about my gramma," she babbled, panicking.

The advancing gator stopped. It shook its head, side to side, then let out a bellowing roar Del could feel in her chest. A rustle came from the thick tufts of seagrass lining the edge of the marsh. Thundering footsteps grew closer, closer. The sun was bright on Del's face, but she couldn't— wouldn't—close her eyes. She kept them on the source of the sound. She couldn't move, could barely breathe as the reeds and seagrasses parted.

"Lundy," she breathed.

If it was possible, he looked even bigger than he had when she first saw him. His grayish-black skin stretched for what looked like miles, and his tail seemed so big it could crush a city. He opened his mouth, and it looked big enough to swallow her whole.

Instead of eating her, though, he spoke.

Well?

The words didn't come from Lundy's mouth, but some-how Del heard them all the same. "Y-you . . . you really *can* talk," she said aloud.

Sure can. Lucky for you.

Del's heartbeat was slowly returning to normal, but she stayed on her guard. She sat up straight, then moved into a crouch, in case she needed to get to her feet and run away quickly.

The young'uns over there said you wanted to ask me a question, Lundy continued. *Ask. I got a nap to get back to.*

"Oh, right. I . . . uh . . ." She swallowed. "The librarian told me you might know why my grandmother left this island. It would have been a long time ago, right after she graduated Vesey."

Lundy's head tilted so he could regard Del out of one large yellow eye. The pupil was a vertical black line inside a yellow iris, thin like a cat's in sunny window.

Plenty of people leave here for plenty of reasons.

"My gramma's name is Violet Vesey. Or, it was back then."

For a moment, the slit of Lundy's pupil widened. His mouth snapped shut. There was a rush of air from his nostrils, and his tail flashed back and forth. From the other gators sunning themselves came a chorus of snapping.

It's all right, young'uns, Lundy said, looking at Del closely. *Looks I won't be getting back to my nap soon as I hoped.*

18

Ol' Lundy sighed, and a wave of his breath washed over Del—a potent mixture of sunshine and raw fish. She shuddered and waited for him to speak again, her heart somewhere in her throat.

Violet is your grandmother, hmm? Lundy's voice rasped, hissed out like air leaking from a tire. *Come closer, little chicken. Let me look at you.*

Del's legs felt like they were tied together. Each step she took toward the gator was a struggle, she was so scared.

Yes, I see a little of her in you.

"D-did you know her?"

The gator's mouth opened in a long hiss. *Yesssss. Long*

ago now. You want gossip, little chicken?

"No, I want . . ." What did she want? Lundy's head swished to the side, watching her with one yellow eye. Waiting. "I want to know what happened to make my gramma leave. And it's not just that—she never told me anything about this place. Why would she leave all these stories, all of this magic, behind?"

Ol' Lundy groaned long and low. *Never worked conjure again, hmm? A shame, a shame. Ah, Miss Violet, she was such a talent. Just all round good at witching. You name it, she could do it. I reckon you'll be the same, little chicken.*

Del looked down at her feet. "Not really," she mumbled.

What's that? Speak up.

"I'm nothing like my gramma," Del said, lifting her head. "She was apparently this great conjurer, and . . . I can't even get my broom to listen to me. It took off when we stumbled upon you and your"—she looked around at the congregation of gators—"family. I'm no good at conjure."

Lundy snorted. *How could you know that already? You just learning. What's it been . . . less than a week? Learning magic, like anything else, takes time.*

"But what if . . . what if my gramma was away from the island so long she lost her connection to the magic and because of that, I can never do it well? In books, kids either have magic or they don't."

A tail swish disturbed the crisp reeds surrounding them, sending out a scent of trampled grass and marsh flowers. Del held her breath, waiting for Lundy's response.

Any of those book you reading about Southern conjure magic? Lundy asked.

Del bit her lip. ". . . No."

Anything the sorcells said make you think somebody could lose their ability to conjure because their gramma left it a long time ago?

When Del didn't answer right away, Lundy slapped his tail on the dirt mound they both stood on, sending up a cloud of dust. "No," she admitted.

Well, then. Lundy shuffled around so his head faced the water in the marsh. His eye bulged out at her, then pulled back to normal. *Sounds like you and your gramma got more in common than you think. Both of y'all need some patience.*

Del dropped her head again. It wasn't that easy, she wanted to say. Not being able to work conjure, seeing things around the island no one else could see—none of the other kids who'd known about conjure their whole lives had any of these problems. Even Gramma hadn't, back when she was here. Everyone kept telling Del this island was her heritage, and these were her people, but she felt even more alone here. Disconnected, somehow.

But she didn't think Lundy would understand that.

She felt something under her chin, lifting her head up.

It was the tip of Lundy's tail, surprisingly gentle. *Unless your ability to conjure ain't really what you worried about.*

"I . . ." Del stopped and thought about Lundy's words before speaking. "My mom died when I was being born, my dad is thousands of miles away, and now my gramma is sick." She swallowed hard and closed her eyes for a moment. "What if something happens to her? She could die, and I'm not even there to be with her. I'm here, learning about a bunch of magic I can't even do, and a bunch of history that has nothing to do with me, that Gramma left behind a million years ago."

Lundy leaned in even closer, looking her straight in the eye. *So nothing you learned here has got anything to do with who you are right now? Or who your grandmother is?*

Del stared back at him. She understood what he was trying to say. The entire time she'd been here on Nemmine Island, she'd been learning her family's history. She knew some of the folktales her ancestors told, the history of the broom and why it was so important to this magic. She knew when the school was founded and the hard fight to be free from their oppressors. She knew there were beings in the world like Sorcell Nyla, who were partly human and partly of the ocean surrounding them. She knew there was a book that contained the names of everyone who had ever been in the same place as she was, trying to learn a magic and a history that connected them all—through the years, and no matter where those people were now. She knew

214

Gramma had been skilled at broomwork and watergazing, the same things the sorcells were teaching her.

But what Lundy didn't understand was that it didn't feel like she was learning about *her* family—it felt like she was learning about *Gramma's* family. Gramma was the one who grew up here; this island was her home and the people here were her family. And she'd left them. *Del's* family was back in Delaware, in a hospital room. And the only thing Del could do to help her was figure out the answer to the first questions she'd asked Nana Rose after climbing into the boat with her. "If all of this is really my history, why didn't Gramma tell me about it before? And why did she leave and never mention it again?"

Lundy moved back a few steps and grunted. *Your gramma sent you here now, hmm? Then she must believe learning about her family and her history is more important than whatever made her leave and never come back.*

Del sighed. So she wasn't going to get any real answers from Lundy either. "Maybe," she said. "But that doesn't answer my question."

Lundy snorted. *Maybe you're right. You're no good at conjure and this place ain't your home. I'm just an ol' gator, what do I know? As far as why your gramma left, I can't tell you what was in her head. Violet didn't share with me 'cause I'm a surly sort. And she knew Rose and I are friends of a kind.*

Del recalled what she'd overheard Nana Rose saying earlier. "So something happened between them? Did they have a fight? Did Nana Rose ask her to leave?"

Never. Lundy thumped his tail again. *Fighting wasn't their way. Rose always held her feelings close. Violet learned that from her. Your gramma was a wonderful conjurer but a quiet one. Didn't have many friends. Always on her own. Especially after . . .*

"After what?" Del prompted, leaning forward.

Ain't my story to tell, Lundy replied. *You're gonna have to ask Rose. Whether you want to or not.*

That's what Del was afraid he'd say. "I already asked and she told me she doesn't know why Gramma left." Del pushed a stray braid out of her face. "Plus, she's mad at me for sneaking out last night and falling into the pool—"

You fell into a pool? Lundy had a reproachful look in one of his giant yellow eyes.

"It's a long story." Del glanced away for a moment, looking over the reed-lined marsh before turning her attention back to Lundy. "Is there any other way for me to find out what happened to my gramma?"

Lundy was still for a moment; he looked like he was thinking. *Young Violet loved the water. She'd come down here to the marsh, or to the sandy side of the island where I brought you in, by herself. Stay there for hours, sitting by the water, singing her heart out. She was too shy to sing in front of Rose, but the water is a good listener.*

"Really?" Del smiled, thinking of Gramma's voice among the grasses around her.

Sure enough. Songs she wrote herself, mostly. Always carried a little book around with her, and she'd scribble in it from time to time.

Del didn't remember any book among Gramma's things. Not that she was able to look for that long. "Do you know where that book could be now?"

If she didn't take it with her when she left, could still be round here somewheres.

Del's heart beat faster. A secret journal? Even if she couldn't believe everything she'd read in her favorite books, that sounded like a real clue. "How do I find it?"

You asking me where to find a book? Lundy growled. *Do I look like a librarian?*

"The librarian!" Del exclaimed. A second later, her excitement faded. "Except . . . the librarian said they'd searched every accessible room on the grounds, and hadn't found anything in any of the books about why Gramma had left."

Well, good luck, little chicken. Wherever that book is, her heart is in there, all wrapped in seafoam.

"Huh?"

With a swift move of his tail, Lundy stomped toward the deep marsh.

"Wait!" she cried, scrambling up to follow.

The enormous gator turned to look at her. Its eye retreated, pulling back into its socket and one . . . two eyelids closed over it. *It's past my breakfast time, and I can't help you any more than I already have.*

In seconds, he was down off the sun-warmed mound of compacted dirt, over the seagrass, into the marsh, and under the water. Del hurried toward the marsh's edge, but Lundy was already submerged up to the eyes on the top of his head, and swimming away fast. Apparently, food was really important to alligators.

Del sighed, guessing she was on her own yet again to figure this mystery out. She turned around to find the path she'd followed to get here—then froze. She was surrounded by the gators Lundy had called young'uns. They didn't look so young to Del. And even if they had left her alone while she was talking to Ol' Lundy, they definitely didn't look friendly now.

"Um . . . okay," Del said, rubbing her palms on her jeans. "I'm just going to walk between you all now . . ."

As soon as the toe of Del's sneaker left the ground, the nearest gator opened its mouth with a sizzling hiss. Two more snapped their jaws and crawled toward her. She gulped. Lundy *had* said it was past breakfast time. She hoped they didn't eat kids.

What now? Del thought, squinting into the brightness of the morning sun. The only other option was the path Lundy had taken, deeper into the marsh. Between the seagrasses and the rippling water, there was a section of land that looked like she could navigate it.

The patch of land looked like the pan of brownies she sometimes helped Gramma bake. The surface was a little crackly like the sun had baked the mud to a dry path. She could follow it past the gators and around the edge of the island to the sandy shore where Lundy had dropped her off when she'd first arrived here. Then she could head up the path from the beach to the house. It couldn't be that far; she could see the roof from where she stood.

So Del stepped down the compacted mound of dirt toward the marsh, holding her arms out at her sides to keep her balance. She wished she had her broom with her now to use as a walking stick like Nana Rose did. She sighed, realizing that the way her broom treated her was kinda the same way she treated Eva and Nana Rose. Del didn't feel like she knew them well enough to trust them. Her broom might feel the same way about her. She couldn't lie to herself—the idea her broom didn't trust her hurt. But she pushed that hurt down deep. She needed to move forward now.

She steadied herself as she got closer to the drier part of the marsh. Here there were no trees to hold on to for support, even the grasses stopped at the marsh's edge. All that was in front of her was the crackly brownie path, and in the distance, farther than she could skip a stone, was the deeper, murkier waters Lundy had sunk into.

Del looked down at her white T-shirt. She didn't want

to get muddy if she slipped and fell, but this was a desperate situation and she had to hurry. Surely, by now Nana Rose had finished talking with Eva and her mother. Was she looking for Del now? Was Del missing class? One thing Del really missed was her phone. She couldn't even check the time. Groaning, she pulled her braids back from her forehead. Should she keep going? Or try to run back through the gators and take a shorter route back to the house?

It was at that moment the choice was made for her: one of Lundy's young'uns turned its head toward her and growled. Several of the others did too. As a group, they raced forward. Del screeched and ran for it. Down the compacted dirt, to the reed-lined marsh, and along toward pond-shaped land bordering the water. It wasn't long before the hiss of the gators faded.

But the moment Del's feet hit the path, however, she realized she was in trouble. The ground she'd thought was solid . . . wasn't. Her feet broke through the crusty baked brownie top and she sank into the sandy mud below down to her ankles. She tried to pull herself free, but all she succeeded in doing was sinking deeper. She was up to her knees in the marsh's embrace before she could take a deep breath. And the mud was steamy hot, like bathwater. Bathwater that enclosed your legs and make them feel like they were in quick-drying cement.

She shouted for help, but she knew it was no use. There

was no one else out here. Ol' Lundy was nowhere to be seen, and everyone else was probably in class.

Del struggled to get free of the sucking mud and sand surrounding her. But it was no use. It held her fast. She was now up to her knees in this stuff. Stuff that, she now realized, was definitely quicksand.

19

Focus, Del. Focus. You can get out of this. She tried to yank herself free, pulling and tugging with all her strength. The quicksand liquefied for a moment, forming a shallow puddle of water on the surface, then immediately after, thickened even more than before. Now she was up to her waist. What was she going to do? She was going to sink in this mess until it covered her all up and no one would even know she'd been here. What would Nana Rose tell Dad or Gramma about her disappearance? She shouted again, but the wind blew her voice up and away and Del had little hope that any of the kids or sorcells were nearby enough to hear her. She wondered if her broom was closer. But that didn't matter, it wasn't like she could call it to her like Nana Rose could.

Here she was, in trouble, and alone. Again. She smacked both her fists against the layer of mud surrounding her waist and screamed at the top of her lungs in frustration.

"Spiraling again, huh?"

Del looked up at the sound of the amused voice. "Eva?"

Her roommate stood at the edge of the marsh well away from the quicksand and posed with one hand on her hip. "The one and only."

Del was so relieved. "How did you find me?"

"Your broom came and got me." She held up Del's broom in the hand that wasn't holding her own, then frowned. "How'd you get caught up in quicksand?"

"It doesn't matter now, just get me out before it swallows me whole!" Del stretched out her arm to Eva as far as she could, waggling her fingertips.

But Eva only rolled her eyes. "It won't swallow you whole. Quicksand only does that in movies. You're probably already as stuck as you're gonna get."

"That . . . doesn't make me feel better," Del said. Actually, it did—but only a tiny bit. Del looked down at where she was stuck in the muddy stuff. She felt like one of those dolls on top of a birthday cake, shoved into snug

223

layers up to her waist. "Pull me out. Please."

"Okay, first things first: you don't pull someone out of quicksand."

"Then how do I get out?"

"Get horizontal and scissor your legs." Eva put both brooms in one hand and moved the fingers of her other hand back and forth like scissor kicks in gym class. "But do it slowly. You need to do it so water gets in the spaces you're making and loosens up the quicksand. When that happens, you can sort of drag yourself out."

Eva sat on the dry grass with both brooms in her lap, giving Del words of encouragement as she worked her legs back and forth carefully, letting the water on top of the marsh filter down through the quicksand. Slowly but surely, its grip on Del loosened and she was able to crawl—arm over arm—out of what she'd thought was a death trap. It took all the energy she had, but she finally collapsed onto dry ground, breathing hard.

"I thought I was a goner there. If it hadn't been for you—" Del looked up at Eva and saw something in her expression. "What is it?"

"You didn't tell me you were coming out here," Eva said, looking at her hard. "You left while I was in Sorcell Rose's office on purpose, so I couldn't come along."

"Oh," Del muttered, sitting up on the marsh bank and looking down at herself. She was covered foot to chest in mud, and when she'd dragged herself out, she'd lost both her sneakers to the quicksand. Mud was even between her toes.

"Yeah," Eva said, pulling her sandaled feet out of Del's muddy reach. "Why would you do that? We did the chewing gum spell. I've never done that with anyone else. I could be helping you figure out this big, important mystery you've got going on, but you don't tell me anything."

Del wanted to argue with her, but she couldn't. If she had told Eva where she was going and what she was doing, she wouldn't be lying here on the bank of the marsh covered in mud. She was exhausted, scared, and her shoes were gone.

She was too ashamed to say anything, but that didn't matter. Eva had enough words for both of them. "If you have secrets, that's cool and all," she said. "But you put yourself in danger. A lot."

Del frowned. "You're out here too."

"Yeah, because of you." Eva folded her arms over her chest. "At least I know not to walk right into quicksand. What the heck are you doing out here anyway?"

Del opened her mouth, then closed it again. She wanted to tell Eva about Lundy and the information he was supposed to have about Gramma, but she couldn't figure out how to do so without making things worse.

After a minute, Eva lifted her chin and gave Del a

sidelong glance. "Right. Secrets. Fine, keep 'em, if that's what you want. If you'd told me where you're going, I could have warned you to stay away from the marsh."

"I didn't want to you get in trouble for me again. Like with the pool. Sorcell Rose called your mom."

"It was no big deal." Eva waved her hand in a shooing motion. "My mom knows me. She was surprised she didn't get a call earlier."

"Eva—" Del started to say, but her roommate shook her head.

"Look, if you want me to leave you alone to do your searching, fine. But you can't get me to help you figure out clues, then drop me and expect me to go away and not care. That's sometimey."

Del wiped her grubby hands on the only small part of her shirt that was still clean. "What's 'sometimey' mean?"

"It's when you're only friendly during the times it's convenient for you, and not other times."

"I just . . . ," Del muttered, looking for the right words. The sun was already drying the mud on her skin until it looked like Ol' Lundy's. And it itched. With the edge of her fingernail, she pulled up a piece of dried mud from her arm and tossed it to the ground. "I hate being . . . dumb and helpless."

"What was that?" Eva asked, one of her reddish-brown eyebrows raised.

Del pressed her lips together, not wanting to repeat

226

what she'd said. But she had to. Keeping silent to Eva was what had hurt their brand-new friendship and put her in danger . . . twice. Keeping silent was also what Gramma and Nana Rose had done all these years, and if it was true that something had happened between them to drive them apart, it had never healed—and look where they were now.

"I said I hate feeling dumb." Del took a deep breath. "I don't know anything about conjure like you and the others do. I can't even keep the land around me from trying to swallow me up."

"If you weren't so dirty, I'd boop your nose," Eva said. "But this is my favorite short set and that mud stains."

"It won't wash out?"

"No. It's pluff mud. Even after you wash it tons of times, your white shirt will still be sort of brownish-beige."

"Oh nooo," Del groaned. "Maybe bleach will—"

"Nope."

"Maybe Nana Rose has something—"

"Wait a minute." Eva looked at Del sharply. "Sorcell Rose is your nana?"

Oh, right. She hadn't told Eva that either. "Yes," Del admitted. "She's my gramma's mom."

"Sorcell Rose is your great-grandmother, and you never told me?"

"I didn't even know she existed until a few days ago!"

"Wow," Eva whispered, wrapping her arms around her knees. "So, it wasn't just that your gramma never told you about Vesey. She never told you about your family either."

Del bit her lip and nodded.

Eva was silent for a moment. "It all makes sense now. Knowing you're part of a magical family must be really weird for you."

"Not weird, just different." Del cracked a small smile.

Eva didn't smile back. "You aren't dumb, Del. You're new. You've never been here before or even heard about magic before. No one expects you to know everything. Or anything." She drummed her fingers along her knees. "You decided to discover something adults have been keeping secret since before you were born. Did you think you could do that all on your own?"

Del rubbed away another drying piece of mud from her skin. "Kinda, yeah."

"Well, that's the only dumb thing I can think of you doing. Oh, and rejecting my friendship, of course."

"But that means your spell didn't work."

Eva shrugged. "Sometimes spells don't work. It even happens to my mom sometimes. Doesn't mean your conjure is terrible."

Del looked away. That was exactly what it meant.

"Look," Eva said. "You know how to dress yourself, don't you? Pour a drink?"

"Of course!"

"So you've never accidentally put your shirt on inside

out? Or spilled some juice on the kitchen table? Mistakes happen. How can magic be perfect when the people who do it aren't?"

Del had no answer for that.

"Anyway." Eva placed Del's broom on the ground in front of her, then grasped her own broom and stood. "If you're not going to tell me anything about what you're doing out here, then I'm going back in. Morning class will be over soon."

As she watched Eva get up and brush dried grass from her kittens-wearing-headphones short set, Del's mind whirled. She ran her hand tenderly over her broom's bristles, hoping the gesture would let the broom know how grateful she was.

But that wasn't enough. Feelings needed to be expressed.

"Thank you for saving my life."

Her broom moved closer to her arm, swiped gently at the dried mud there. Del cradled it in her lap as she puzzled out what to do next.

Magic wasn't perfect. She'd thought that if she could learn this magic, she'd be able to figure out why Gramma had kept this place a secret, maybe even become a capable conjurer one day. Then she'd finally feel like she belonged somewhere, fix everything broken in her life.

Magic wasn't a cure-all to make a picture-perfect life. It

wouldn't bring her mom back, or magically make Gramma better. But that wasn't the point of Southern conjure. The point of it had been staring her in the face the entire time she'd been here. Nana Rose had even told her that first day. It was to give people living in an imperfect world some peace, some community, and some connection. Even some friendship. The exact things Eva had been offering. And Del needed to give her a chance to trust that friendship. The same chance her broom had given her. Now that she knew better, she had to do better.

Protect. Educate. Survive.

They all needed each other to do that. Del's search for the truth about Nana Rose and Gramma wasn't about fixing herself. It was about helping *them* connect once again. And that's what she needed to do, *especially* if they were too stubborn to do it themselves.

"Eva, wait," she called.

Del stood, tucked her broom under her arm. Looking down at her bare feet, she said, "I'm sorry I didn't trust you before. I'm always the new kid at school and I'm not used to making friends. Or anyone wanting to help me. I guess I was afraid you were too good to be true. I never meant to hurt you." She looked up. "But I promise to try harder to trust from now on."

Eva's smile was the brightest Del had ever seen it. Only this time she didn't squint at the rose-gold brightness from her braces. This time, Del returned the smile.

"I told you my spell worked," Eva said, nudging Del's shoulder with one finger. "And it's a good thing it did. There was no way you gonna solve this mystery without me anyways."

20

On the way back to the house, Del finally told Eva everything about what was happening between Nana Rose and Gramma and the mystery she was trying to solve. She also filled Eva in on what she learned from the librarian and the information about the diary Lundy had given her.

When they got back, the other kids were just leaving morning classes. They stared at Del's mud-covered clothes and bare feet, but she ignored them. All she wanted to do was sneak past Nana Rose, have a shower, and maybe rest a little before she and Eva figured out their next steps.

They made their way past their classmates and toward the main staircase.

"May I see you in my office, Del?"

With a start, Del turned to find Nana Rose had appeared in the front room. Her expression was stern. "Okay," she managed to say. Eva gave her a sympathetic look as Del trudged up the stairs behind her great-grandmother.

Once in Nana Rose's office, Del chose to stand. She couldn't sit on any of the chairs because she might stain them with the mud still clinging to her skin and clothes.

"Just because I chose to speak to Eva first doesn't mean you get away without a talking to. But it seems like the pool isn't all we need to talk about." Nana Rose looked her up and down. "Where have you been? Did you go out to the marsh? You're a mess!"

Del wanted to explain that she was only looking for answers to questions Nana Rose herself wouldn't answer. Things even Gramma was hiding from her in that blue briefcase of hers. But she knew that wasn't Nana Rose's point. She shouldn't have done something so dangerous. Twice. So she just nodded. "I did go out to the marsh this morning. I'm sorry." She decided not to mention being chased by gators, and getting stuck in quicksand.

Her great-grandmother let out a long breath. "I'm sure you know what I'm going to say. You're my responsibility this summer. Which means you need to be responsible as well. You should know better than to sneak around the house at night in dangerous areas like the pool. And while the school grounds are open to all the students of Vesey, you must use your common sense when it comes to exploring areas that are off the main pathways. If you're going to visit the marsh"—she wrinkled her nose—"take care to not lose your footing. Do you understand?"

Del nodded again. All she wanted to do was get out of that room.

Nana Rose dropped into the chair behind her huge wooden desk. "Be safe. Use your brain and think before doing things. Lord, it's been a long time since I had to deal with such a willful child. First your grandmother, always off by the water scribbling in her journal when she should have been studying, and now you running around here without any heed to—"

"Her journal?" That caught Del's attention. Maybe finding it was going to be easier then she'd thought. "I didn't know she had a journal. Would it still be here, somewhere?"

She waved her hand. "That was ages and ages ago." She stared at Del for a moment, looking like she wanted to say more, but she just sighed. "Well, go on, then. I'm sure you're eager to clean off that itchy mud. No classes for you and Eva for the rest of today. But I would like you to use the time to study on your own."

Del nodded and trudged out of Nana Rose's office.

Eva raised an eyebrow at her when she got back to their room, but Del didn't say anything yet. After a shower and a change of clothes, though, she felt tons better. Jube brought up lunch on trays for them both, giving them a sympathetic look before he faded way.

Once he was gone, Del sat on her bed and eyed Eva, who was focused on her sketchpad. "What are you doing?"

"Going over my sketch again," she replied. "The one I made of Vesey. Old houses like this can have hidden compartments and such. It made me wonder if there's a place your gramma might have hidden things."

"Seriously?" Del asked. "Why didn't you tell me this before?"

"Because I didn't know you were looking for anything until a little while ago." Eva raised an eyebrow.

Del winced. "Oh, yeah."

Eva grinned at her before scratching her pencil along the paper, measuring with her ruler. "And yes. Lots of old house have secret rooms and passages. Some of them were built on purpose, as escape routes. And my dad told me once that people back in the day used to seal up rooms they didn't need anymore, so that the houses would be easier to heat and stuff."

Del smeared lotion on her arms, legs, and feet. That dunk in the marsh mud had dried her skin out badly. One of her braids came out of her scrunchie, and she tucked it back while she rolled Eva's words over and over in her mind. *Old houses can have secret rooms. Built for a specific purpose, or sealed off because they were empty.*

"You know how Ol' Lundy said Gramma had a diary and it might still be here?" When Eva nodded, Del continued. "If Nana Rose sealed up Gramma's old bedroom, maybe the diary is in there."

For once, Eva was more cautious than Del expected. "Could be," she murmured. "But didn't the librarian say they'd searched every book in the house? That would include a journal your gramma would have left behind."

Del opened and closed her mouth. Her heart sank as she realized Eva was right.

Eva continued, "She could have taken it with her, and it's in that memory briefcase you mentioned."

Del hadn't thought about that, and it made her heart sink even further. After all the mistakes and mishaps and trouble she'd gotten herself into, could it be that the truth about this school, about Del's family legacy, was in Gramma's memory case? So close to Del for her entire life? How many times had she asked to know about her family, about Gramma's life? The people she was related to? Now she was finally in a place where she ask those questions properly, and the answers were all back home.

She let out a cry of frustration and anger and flopped back down on her bed.

"Hey, hey." Eva reached over and shook her arm gently. "I'm sorry. I didn't mean to upset you. I was just trying to keep you from getting your hopes up. But that's not what you need right now."

"It's okay," Del replied, not moving.

"No, it isn't. You trusted me enough to share your family secrets and worries. You didn't need Reality-Check-Eva. What you needed was Super-Supportive, We-Can-Do-This-Eva." Her roommate's scratching and scribbling on her sketchbook resumed, more frantic than before. "Even if the journal isn't here, it's possible there's a secret room in the house, one your Gramma knew about. And if there is, it might have answers, even if her journal isn't there. We just need to figure out how to access it."

Del shot up in bed. *Access.* The librarian had said the search for books with information about Violet Vesey included all *accessible* rooms on the property. But what if Gramma's old bedroom wasn't accessible? That would mean there could be a book in there. . . .

"Eva!" Del said. "You're a genius!"

"I know." She smirked.

"No, I mean that you might have figured out how the journal could be here after all. Remember what the librarian said? About all *accessible* rooms on the property being searched?"

Eva's eyes went wide, connecting the clues immediately. "All right, now we *have* to figure out if there are any secret rooms here."

"Where would we even start looking?" Del asked.

"There must be twenty rooms that *aren't* hidden in this place."

Eva didn't look up from her sketchpad, but Del could hear her pencil tapping along the page. "I think it's actually thirty rooms."

"Ugh." She fell back on the bed again. "Right now we could use a miracle."

Del felt the bed dip behind her head and a moment later Eva's upside-down face appeared above hers. She yelped in shock at the sight of her up so close, then frowned.

"Cheer up!" her roommate said. "It isn't a miracle, but I think I've figured out where the hidden room might be."

"What? How?"

She held out the drawing she'd done of the house on their first day. "In looking at the house again on our walk back from the marsh, I noticed some of the rooms don't really line up with the arrangement of rooms in the interior of the house. Look."

Del took the sketchbook. It was a pretty impressive drawing of the front of the house, complete with the column-lined porch, front door, and the many, many windows. Del turned the page and found Eva had started on the back and sides of the house as well but the drawings weren't complete.

"What am I supposed to be looking at?" Del asked.

Eva sat on the bed next to Del. "Here," she said. "This is the front door. We've got three floors." She pointed to an opening on the second floor of the big square drawing. "Look at the number of windows. There's usually the same number of windows on the left side of the house as the right side. On the left: one, two, three, four windows. Here . . ."

"There's only three!" Del exclaimed.

"Yep. Weird, right?"

"Do you think there's a room there and they just covered up the window?"

"One way to find out," Eva said, springing up from the bed and heading to the door.

The hallway was quiet, with the other kids in afternoon class. Del once again noticed the paintings lining the walls; the one closest to her was of the footpath leading to the flower garden. It was lush and full of color, as everything was in bloom.

"Now look at this whole hallway. See anything weird?" Eva held her palm out, moving it left and right.

Del glanced up and down the hall, feeling the weight of Eva's expectant stare. "There are four bedrooms on the right side and only three on the left. So . . . there might be a hidden room where the fourth bedroom should be?"

"You got it!"

"But . . . that's where Nana Rose's bedroom and office are. Could be that those rooms take up the same space as one of the bedrooms."

"Could be," Eva admitted. "Could be something else, though."

239

"So how do we find out?"

Eva's eyes were bright. "We sneak in."

Del hesitated. She just got a talking to from Nana Rose about this exact thing. Plus, she hated having to sneak around to find out things she felt she had a right to know. But she knew there were things Nana Rose wasn't telling her, things she herself might not even know.

And besides, she had a partner now.

"Okay," Del agreed.

"Cool. Now how do we get into her office?"

"Why are you asking me?"

"She's your great-grandmother?"

"You've known her longer than I have!" Del groaned. "This is going to be harder than I thought."

Eva twisted the straw in her earlobes. "Don't spiral. We'll figure it out. Maybe we can wait until she leaves?"

Del shook her head. "We could be waiting here forever. We need to find a way to get her out of the room."

"Like a diversion." Eva thought for a moment. "Too bad we don't have any chickens."

Del let out a laugh. "Chickens? That's your first thought?"

Eva stuck her nose up in the air. "Chickens are very distracting. And they're faster than you think they are."

"Well, we don't have any chickens. So we need something else." Del wished she could use her phone to look up "convenient distractions." Surely someone had made a list of good ones somewhere. But her phone didn't have a signal and was of no use. Unless . . .

Del retrieved her phone from her backpack and pressed a button. It still couldn't find a signal, but there was plenty of battery left. "I think I have a plan."

"What kind of plan?"

Del pressed another button and Eva's voice came through the phone. *What kind of plan?*

"You recorded me?"

"Shh! That's the idea."

Eva nodded, like she was starting to understand. "So what's your plan?"

Del told Eva about how her broom had tugged her through the house and to the side door that led out to the boathouse. "And you already know it came to get you when I was in the marsh. I'm thinking we record ourselves talking about going back to the marsh, something like that, then tie the phone to my broom and tell—I mean *ask* it to stay hidden, so Nana Rose has to keep following it, looking around for us."

A heartbeat passed before Eva replied. "Will your broom do it?"

"I don't know." Del smoothed the broom's bristles. "Will you?"

The broom flipped over on Del's lap, which she took to be a yes. Del hit record, and after a few takes, they had their distraction.

"What do you think?"

Eva shrugged her approval. "It's not chickens, but it's pretty good."

Del rolled her eyes and laughed as she secured her phone to her broom. "We've got about fifteen minutes of us talking. It's on repeat so Nana Rose will probably figure it out after it loops around once or twice. We'll have to hurry."

"I'm ready," Eva said, buckling her sandals on.

After a brief chat to her broom, Del pressed the button to play the recording she and Eva made. "There's a short delay before the recording starts to give my broom time to get down the hall to Nana Rose's room."

Del and Eva hid under their beds as Del's broom went about its work. They left the door to their room open to see when their opportunity would appear. Their recording began and they both held their breath. Soon, Del's broom moved past their room, staying close to the shadows. A few moments later, the door to Nana Rose's office opened and the sound of footsteps shuffled past the open door.

"Girls? What are you up to?"

Del and Eva waited until Nana Rose's footsteps faded away down the stairs before they crawled out of their hiding place.

"Okay, let's go!" Del said.

Quietly as they could, they left their bedroom, Eva with her broom and sketchpad and Del with her fingers crossed. No one was around. Even so, the girls peeked left and right to make sure they were alone on the second floor of the house.

"Hurry."

"I'm right behind you," Eva said, tiptoeing to the large wooden door at the end of the hall. "How are we going to get in, though?"

Del looked up at the imposing dark wood door. It was similar to the one at the front of the house, carved with intricate images of brooms, interspersed with corn and rice and what she now knew to be sorghum. "Maybe it's unlocked?"

When Eva tried to turn the knob it wouldn't budge. "Nope. And she probably took the key with her. Maybe there's a spell for unlocking? I could look it up."

"That might take a long time." Del tapped her finger against her bottom lip.

"Well, we can't break the door down. Can you pick a lock?" Eva nervously glanced back toward the staircase.

"No, but I have an idea." She began examining the paintings in the hallway. "Remember Sorcell Harus, and his lessons on rituals? My gramma always hides spare keys behind pictures, just in case we get locked out of a room and she loses her keys. I wonder if she learned that trick from her own mother." Del felt behind the painting closest to them. Nothing.

Eva came over to help. Together, they moved down

the row of paintings, Eva carefully lifting the frames away from the wall just enough for Del to get her arm behind them to feel around for a key. On the very last painting before the staircase, Del felt it. She had to jump to push the key off the tiny hook it rested on. The key fell to the carpet without a sound.

"Gotcha!" Del said, grabbing it from the floor.

"Let's hope it's the right key."

They ran back down the hall. Del fed the key into the lock and turned it. With a click, the door opened.

"Daggone," Eva said, impressed.

Del grinned. "I guess you don't need magic for everything. Come on!"

21

The girls entered Sorcell Rose's office. The large room was bordered on two sides with floor-to-ceiling windows. It felt different standing in this room without her great-grandmother here—gentler, it seemed, when it wasn't filled with her intense presence and magic. A carved wooden desk stood in the center of the room, covered in stacks of papers that were held down with polished rocks and crystals of different sizes, colors, and textures. Woven bowls filled with an assortment of pens, pencils, paper clips, and rubber stamps adorned one of its corners. A thick braided rug covered most of the floor. Along the wall with the main door stood bookcases filled with large hardcover books and an assortment of scrolled papers tied with cord. A light, floral fragrance hung in the room, as if a scented candle burned somewhere out of sight. On the opposite end of the room stood a closed door that, Del guessed, led to Nana Rose's bedroom.

"What do we do now?" she asked.

Eva pressed her lips together and consulted her sketch-book. "This is where the connections to the hidden room should be, along this wall somewhere." She strolled to the far left corner of the room, running her hand all along the wall as she went. "I don't see any place that looks boarded up or patched up, though."

"Maybe you didn't get the sketches right?" Del suggested.

Eva gave Del a *look*.

Del held her hands up. "Just asking."

"Could be, I guess," Eva admitted. "But I don't think so. This wall is the only one without framed pictures or a bookshelf. Just this big plant. Here, help me move it."

Del pulled while Eva pushed and they managed to get the huge potted plant away from the wall. "Now what?"

Eva pressed her ear against the wall and knocked on it. "I've seen my dad do this. He says you can tell what's behind a wall this way. If there's a room beyond, it'll sound hollow, like when you tap on a ripe watermelon."

Del tapped the walls like Eva had, but she'd never listened to the inside of a ripe watermelon so she wasn't sure what she was listening for. "Um . . . is there anything else we can try? We don't have a lot of time."

Eva scanned the entire wall from floor to ceiling. "Look for differences in the color of the paint. The hue can change when it's applied to different materials. Different textures on the wall."

"Okay." Del stepped back from the wall. There weren't any of the indicators Eva mentioned. "I don't see anything."

"Me either," Eva admitted. "It looks like whoever boarded it up did a really good job." Eva started running her hands over the wall. "See if you feel anything to push or press that might reveal a door?"

The girls pushed and prodded the wall, searching for any way to get beyond it. She shoved hard against the barrier with both hands. Nothing moved.

"Maybe it's sealed up so there's no way to get in without destroying the wall," Eva said.

"And we can't do that."

"Ugh," Del groaned. She turned her back to the wall and slid down it. She placed her head in her hands and inhaled a deep breath through her nose, then blew it out through her mouth. What was that smell? Del sniffed again, trying to hold the air in her lungs long enough to determine what the fleeting scent was. She recognized it from her time here on the island, but couldn't place it.

"The marsh!" she shouted, startling Eva who was investigating at the other end of the wall.

"Shh! We're supposed to be sneaking around right now, remember?"

"Right, right." Del got up and kneeled next to the wall, pressing her nose against it. "I can smell something, kinda like the mud I was covered in, coming from here."

"Pluff mud?" Eva asked, joining her.

"That's it. And it's coming from this specific corner."

Eva tapped her finger against her lip. "Maybe the door isn't boarded up at all. Sorcell Rose could have used magic to conceal the door. Where is the odor strongest? That might be the hinge of the door or the gap underneath it."

Del ran her hand along the base of the wall where the marsh's scent had come through, and a slight air movement touched her palm. She pushed against the section where the air leaked out, hoping to find a way in. No luck. Frustrated, she stood and slapped her palm against the wall, generating a click followed by the groan of what sounded like an ancient machine. Musty air whooshed through the room, invading the summer-sweet fragrance hovering in Nana Rose's office.

"Whoa," Del said, almost losing her balance. She looked up at the wall that had been solid only a few moments before. "Whoa," she repeated.

An opening yawned in the wall—door-size but circle-shaped, like a portal in a sci-fi movie. It was clearly made with magic, the doorway dark and shimmering, hiding what was on the other side. Del shivered.

Eva stared nervously at the opening. "Seems stupid not to go through now that we found it." She bit her lip. "What do you think?"

The opening in the wall had an energy all its own, a pulsing, living feeling that made the hairs on the back of Del's neck prickle. Exactly like the magic that ran through the island itself.

"But we don't know what—or who—is in there." The shadowy presence had to be here on this island somewhere, and Del was still on guard. Especially since she might be the reason it was even here.

Eva clutched her broom in her fist. "I'm not good at fighting, but if anything happens in there I'll do my best."

Del wished she had her broom. If she hadn't used her phone to create the distraction in the elevator, she could use it as a flashlight. But she would have to go without either of them. "Why are we so worried? What could be in there?" Del said with a confidence she didn't exactly feel.

Eva raised an eyebrow, but didn't answer.

No sound came from the room. It was eerily silent and still. After a long gaze into the portal, Del said, "Here we go."

The girls walked side by side through the portal. Del felt a shiver pass over her, like walking through a mist, but only for a moment, and then they were on the other side.

Like Nana Rose's room, this one also had floor-to-ceiling windows, but they'd been covered over. There was no need to worry about light as a soft glow filled the room, like moonlight or like the orbs of light that floated up over the marsh at nighttime. Del didn't know where it was coming from, but it must have been magic. With the room lit enough to see, they surveyed the entire area.

A neatly made bed covered in a hand-crocheted blanket stood against the far wall. A desk and chair sat to its left and a dresser to its right. All of it should've been coated with a layer of dust and dirt from years of disuse, but it wasn't—it seemed as though someone had recently cleaned.

Del picked up a silver frame from the dresser and studied the picture. It was of a smiling young woman smiling sitting on the steps of a building, a stack of books next to her.

"This looks like where we have classes." She turned the frame toward Eva.

"That's 'cause it is." Eva was analyzing a trophy of some kind when she glanced at the photo Del held out. "Look at the shape of the roof in the background."

Del twisted the picture to see the detail. The young woman in the picture looked familiar as well. Even though the face was younger and the clothing and hairstyle old-fashioned, she would recognize that smile anywhere. "This is my grandmother," she said, squinting as light reflected off the frame. As she looked closer, she could tell that while Gramma was smiling, there was a sadness behind it.

Del gazed around. Never did she think she'd be in

here, where her grandmother grew up. It looked like a regular girl's bedroom. What had Del expected? Her gramma had been a girl here, not much older than Del was now. While this room looked normal, it felt different. It felt—Del closed her eyes and let the sensation run over her—alive. The same vibration of power she'd felt when Nana Rose and the sorcells had captured the wild boar stampede, she felt now. It was gentler, like it had been sleeping, but Del could sense it all the same. Sleeping, or . . . waiting. Del shuddered. What would happen once it woke up?

Eva read out the information on the trophy she was holding, breaking the silence. "First place, Broomwork: Violet Vesey."

"That's my grandmother." Del crept over and carefully took the trophy from Eva, feeling its heavy weight. "Why was this room magically sealed? It's like someone wanted to erase the fact she had ever been here."

"But there's no dust, so they still come in here to clean." Eva met Del's confused gaze. She gestured at the walls. "Recognize the paint color?"

"Seafoam green," Del said, turning in a full circle. "Lundy said the diary was *wrapped in seafoam.*"

Eva wandered around the room, her sandals scuffing on the wood floor. "I can feel the magic in here."

"So can I."

The floor creaked and both girls looked up, fear

251

freezing them to the spot as the portal flickered once, then was still. Eva held her broom up, ready to swing at whatever emerged from the swirling portal. Del held up the trophy already in her hand, the memory of the night her gramma went to the hospital sparking bright in her memory. Heart hammering, she waited along with Eva at her side.

But nothing came through the opening.

After a few moments, they relaxed, looked at each other, and laughed awkwardly at their fear. Eva went to the chifforobe and opened the door. Del went to the dresser and opened each drawer, sifting through the clothes and objects she found. It was like time had stopped in this room when her grandmother had left it. She could hear Eva scraping hangers over the metal bar inside the chifforobe, making the furniture echo with its emptiness.

"There isn't much here," her friend said, going over to the bookcase. She plucked books from the shelves and flipped through the pages before replacing them.

"The diary has to be here somewhere," Del said, crouching to yank open the final drawer. Inside lay the same dress her grandmother was wearing in the picture where she had a smile that didn't reach her eyes. Del wondered if the picture had been taken right before she decided to leave the island. If so, that could be why she had left this dress behind. She wanted to shed the memories of this place as she left to find a new home. Del knew what that felt like.

She tried to push the drawer back in, but it stuck and

wouldn't slide back, so Del pulled it out all the way to reset it. She kneeled down to reach into the empty space where the drawer was to see what was preventing it from closing.

That's when she felt something. Wedged in the bottom of that empty space was a slim book. Del drew it out of its hiding spot. Like the rest of the room, there was no dust or dirt on it.

Del sat on the bed with it, and Eva joined her. "That's gotta be it," she whispered.

"I think so too," Del agreed. She turned it over in her hand, and found a small lock holding it shut. "How do we open it? Did you spot a key anywhere?"

"That's a permission lock," Eva told her. "It's a spell."

Every minute Del spent here, there was something new to learn. "How do you open a permission lock?"

"Ask it. Politely. It'll decide if it should open for you."

Del wiped her palms on her shorts. Cradling the diary gently in her lap, she said, "Will you please unlock for me?"

Why?

The voice of a young girl seemed to come from the diary itself. Del was so surprised she almost dropped it. She looked at Eva who nodded, not surprised at all.

"Permission locks usually have questions before they'll open. Just tell the truth."

This was one of the strangest experiences she ever had. "I want to read you."

Why?

"I want to find out why my grandmother left this island so many years ago. And why she didn't take you with her," Del added.

There was a pause. Then, *Who are you?*

"Violet Vesey's granddaughter."

The pause the lock gave was longer this time. *I am Violet's diary.*

"I know," Del whispered. "That's why I'm here."

How is Violet?

"She's . . . sick."

This was the longest pause yet. Del was nervous, but she tried her best to stay calm and not make the diary anxious. Next to her Eva was statue-still, and the only other sound in the room was their breathing.

A soft click and the lock opened, and a piece of paper fluttered to the floor and lay at their feet.

Del picked it up. The paper itself was torn and creased as if it had been stashed away many times and then reopened and smoothed out. When Del unfolded it, she saw it was an advertisement for backup singers for a band touring the East Coast, with longer performances in New York City, Atlantic City, and Philadelphia. They would provide clothes, food, and lodging on top of a payment per show.

"Do you think Gramma could've left home because of this?" Del held out the paper.

Eva set her sketchbook down on the nightstand and plucked the advertisement from her roommate's fingers.

"Maybe. Look at the date. How old would your grand-mother have been in 1977?"

Gramma's song "Not Another Day" came out in 1979, when she was nineteen years old. Del had read that on one of those historical music review sites. "Um . . . she would've been seventeen? That would have been when she was close to graduating. . . ."

"I can't imagine wanting a job that would take me that far away, all alone without any friends or family," Eva said, shaking her head. "I mean, it sounds scary." She handed the paper back to Del.

The situation sounded a little like the one she was in. She was far away from home and when she left her house, she didn't know what Nana Rose or the school or the other people were going to be like. While Del had been forced to come to Vesey, her gramma had chosen to go on this new adventure. She turned to the first page of the journal.

> *March 17, 1972*
> *I won, I won, I won!*
> *Watergazing champion of the year is Violet Vesey! I can't believe it. I got a gold medal just like Wilma Rudolph got in the 1960 Summer Olympics and it's so cool. I won't wear it, though, it'll stay in the box in my top drawer. (Okay, I just wore it once.)*
> *Maybe I'll write a song about today. Or maybe I'll just shout about it in this diary!*

*Pop is taking me fishing and we're going to cook
dinner for Mom. She's been working so hard on
raising enrollment for next year. But I'm sure we'll
have plenty of new students. Vesey Conservatory is the
best—and I'm not just saying that because my name is
on it!*

"She sounds like fun," Eva said, reading over Del's
shoulder.

"Yeah, she does."

Del turned to the next page to find a detailed description of the dinner Gramma and her dad prepared for Nana
Rose and how much she appreciated their effort. They
took pictures and played cards that night before bed. It
sounded perfect to Del.

She flipped forward, about a quarter of the way through
the book.

*January 1, 1973
Happy New Year!
I know I haven't written a lot lately, but it's a new
year and my resolution is to write more here. I have
a different notebook that I'm using to write songs in,
that's where I've been doing most of my writing (I
hope you're not offended, diary). I'm not that good
yet, and I have to use a rhyming dictionary and a*

thesaurus sometimes, but I'll get better. I love singing other people's songs but I want to write my own, y'know? Of course you do, you're my diary!

I asked Mom if I could wear some of her lipstick, but she said thirteen was too young for makeup. I'll be fourteen in September and I can't wait! Anyway, I'm looking forward to a great year. Will write more later.

On the very next page, it read:

October 30, 1974

Okay, so I didn't keep my resolution to write more. I'm sorry! I've been busy. Not really, I just forgot. But I have news. Guess who won the Best Broomworker title at the All Saints' Day Carnival?

Me!

Miss Heath from Sea Island Magic Academy presented me with a trophy and Mom and Pop jumped up and down, cheering at the ceremony. I was so embarrassed! Ha! Sort of, but not really. But it was nice to have a day out with Mom and Dad, all three of us together. Mom's always so busy during the school year . . . Kids from Vesey won some other prizes too. For watergazing (Maxine beat me—but I'm happy for her!) and for candlemaking. The ones from Nature Academy this year were TERRIBLE.

"It sounds like she was really happy here. . . ." Eva said.

"Yeah," Del replied. She found a satin bookmark sewn into the diary and lifted it up, opening the book to the marked area. There were several pages torn out, leaving jagged alligator-teeth edges.

She felt Eva lean closer to read the next page, where the handwriting wasn't as neat.

November 9, 1975

I don't know what to write here. Already I tried three or four times and nothing sounded right so I ripped those pages out. Nothing sounds right anymore and it's been months. Six months and seventeen days exactly and she still won't talk to me about it. He's gone and she doesn't even care. All she talks about is the school. Violet, help me make some new brooms. Violet, I need to you to paint one of the rooms. Violet, you're in charge of candlemaking club now that Cece's graduated.

Know what Mom did over the summer, instead of us going on our usual family trip? She started a summer session. All through July and August we had students here when it used to be our time to do things together. And she just scheduled me to help. Without even talking to me about it.

I wish there were some magic that could fix her.
Or take me away from here.

Del was right—something had happened between
Gramma and Nana Rose. *He's gone and she doesn't even
care . . .* Who was Gramma talking about?

Del flipped the page. There were only a few more hast-
ily scribbled entries:

> *May 14, 1976*
> *I never really write in here anymore. There's
> nothing new to say.*

> *October 29, 1976*
> *I told her I'm not going to the All Saints' Day
> Carnival. She wasn't happy but she couldn't make me
> go. I've put up with this silence too long already.*

> *February 9, 1977*
> *I wrote a song today. It's just a draft but it helped
> me figure a lot of things out. That's what I needed, I
> guess.*

"That's the last entry?" Eva asked.

Del nodded. "I wonder if the song she's talking about
is 'Not Another Day.' If that's the case, maybe Gramma's

boyfriend left the school and Nana Rose expected her to get over it?" Del closed the diary. "It's just a guess, but that's what her song's about."

"Seems like a lot of mess for a boyfriend . . . but what do I know?" Eva said. "Maybe her mom didn't want her to be a singer. It sounds like Sorcell Rose wanted her to take on more responsibility. Maybe she wanted your gramma to take over running the school someday? And your gramma left because she didn't want to?"

"Could be." Del opened the small nightstand drawer. It was empty except for lining paper printed with tiny roses and vines. The faint smell of flowers blossomed from the drawer. "Whatever it was, Gramma didn't get along with Nana Rose afterward."

Del sat the book down on the bed, causing a rustle from beneath the bed covers. She jumped back and Eva squeaked as the covers flew forward as if someone kicked them off. A blur flew up from the bed, a streak that Del couldn't see clearly.

"What is that?" Eva yelped, ducking and covering her head with one hand.

The streak flew by again. "It's a broom!" Del said. The broom whizzed erratically by their heads again. Then it stopped, hovering at the ceiling. "It . . . must've been my gramma's."

"What are you going to do?" Eva asked, clutching her

own broom tight under her arm as the broom circled the room again.

Del whispered out the side of her mouth so only Eva could hear. "I'm gonna get it."

Eva's mouth dropped open but she promptly shut it and gulped. "I'll help."

"Block the way out with your broom and I'll try to—"

Before Del could finish speaking, the broom dove from the ceiling toward the bed. As Del poised to spring for the handle, the broom curved its path, turning and heading for the exit.

"Catch it! We can't let it get out of this room!"

Eva ran for the portal. Del grabbed the crocheted blanket from the bed and followed. With Eva blocking the door, the broom circled back the way it came, diving under the bed and out the other side. It turned up sharply and skimmed along the ceiling. The top of the portal door was low and the broom dipped and shot for the exit, handle first.

Del saw her chance. She flicked the blanket like her dad's barber flicked the cape to clear it of all the stray hairs. The blanket flew up and then settled down heavily on the bristles of the broom, pinning it to the floor with a soft whoosh.

"Yes, you got it!" Eva whooped.

Before the broom could free itself, Del took it by the

handle. A jolt of power went through her fingers, up her arm, and radiated in her chest. She gasped and toppled backward, but she kept her grip on the wooden handle. It was like nothing else she'd ever felt before. Like a cloak wrapping her up on a chilly day, or like a rope around her waist when she was clinging to the edge of a cliff. It felt like a connection . . . a bond. And it felt . . . good?

"That was amazing!" Eva said, but Del could barely hear it. The power surge she felt from touching the broom for the first time was easing up and she was beginning to think properly again.

"Did you feel something when you touched your broom for the first time?" she asked, breathlessly.

Eva swallowed, then nodded. "I felt comfortable. Like I could trust it somehow."

"That's what this feels like," Del said, putting one hand on Eva shoulder. Her other hand clutched the new-found broom.

It was surprisingly quiet, and not trying to flee any-more. It was an unusual looking broom, taller than she was and made of red, polished wood. The bristles were light brown and black, and braided together with blue cord, but they were frayed into softness and slightly bent at the ends, unlike the straight ones on Eva's brand-new broom. If the ends of her hair had looked the same as her broom she would have said she needed a trim. But this broom seemed right just as it was. It was *definitely* her gramma's broom.

Del took a deep breath, enjoying the spark of connection. Still, this wasn't her broom. Maybe she could return it to Gramma, if she recovered soon.

Eva tapped her on the arm. "Del?"

"Huh? Oh, wow."

The pages of the diary moved as if turned by some unseen hand. They turned slowly, as if someone licked their finger first to get a grip on the page, then carefully turned it and smoothed it down before moving to the next page.

Then the chair at the desk pulled out and turned around. As the girls stared, a dark shadowy shape like the one Del had been seeing since the failed protection spell formed in the chair.

"Maybe I can answer some of your questions, Delphinia."

22

Del and Eva shrieked.

"I told you I saw something!" Del cried. She was about to sprint for the portal when she realized the diary was still on the other side of the room. Next to the shadow thing. She didn't want to leave it behind.

Eva bravely held up her broom. "I don't know what you are, but—"

"I'm the reason Violet left the island," the shadow said sadly. "At least, one of them."

Del exhaled, cautiously. The shadow's gentle tone and the easy way it sat in the chair drained away her fear. "Who are you?" she asked.

"Robert Vesey. Bobby." The shadow let out a slow exhale that brought a rush of chilled air into the room.

That name was familiar. Where had Del heard it before? *The library.* While she had focused on Violet Vesey's entry in the book that recorded all the school's students, there was a name that had been written on the spine: Robert Vesey.

"You compiled all the student names in the book in the library," Del said.

"That I did."

"So you must be related to Del," Eva said.

"I'm her great-grandfather. Violet's father. Or, I was." The shadow's head tilted. "Hm . . . I suppose I still am."

"If you are my great-grandad, why didn't you just tell me instead of sneaking around all ghostily?"

"'Ghostily'?" Eva snorted.

"You know what I mean, Eva." Del huffed.

The shadowy Vesey laughed softly. "I didn't mean to scare you, but I didn't have the strength to appear to you the way I am now. It's been years since I've been able to set foot on this island and draw enough energy from it to appear."

"You died here? Don't ghosts usually haunt the place where they die?"

"They can, unless they have a special reason to move around. I died while fishing in my boat on the water, away from the island. So when I wanted to return home as a ghost, I couldn't get through the island's protection spell. For so many years, I was alone, getting weaker and weaker, unable to communicate with my daughter or my wife."

"Nana Rose?"

The shadow solidified more. Robert Vesey was less like a smear, and more like a person in silhouette. "Yes. I knew she'd like that name the moment you gave it to her."

"You heard that?" Del asked.

A slow nod. "I heard all of what you said in the boat on the way here. Your worries and doubts, how dearly you wanted to know why Violet left, and why she never mentioned this place. I knew had to try to get back on Nemmine. And when the protection spell was weakened, that was my chance."

Del hung her head. "That was because of me."

Eva looked at her. "What do you mean?"

"I didn't help perform the protection spell at the cook-out," she said. "I messed up. The boar attack was my fault."

"It's okay," Eva said after a moment. She nudged against Del gently with her arm. "Everyone makes mistakes sometimes. Even I do, as amazing as I am."

With great effort, Del met Eva's gaze. She had promised not to hide things anymore. Eva's acceptance of her good and bad points was really helping with that. "I didn't believe conjure was real that first day. I thought this whole magic thing was silly. So I stayed silent when everyone else recited the spell. Even if the magic was 'real,' I suppose I didn't think it mattered if one person didn't join in."

Eva nodded. "It's not about how many people there are to perform a spell like that. It's about everyone in the circle doing it together."

Del held her grandmother's broom, its energy warming her arms. "Maybe that's why my broom didn't trust me at first."

"Well, Del," Robert Vesey said, "I'm thankful for your moment of disbelief. Otherwise, I wouldn't have been able to return home." His voice held sadness and regret that tugged at Del's heartstrings. "I wish I could have returned earlier and talked to Violet. Maybe what happened could have been avoided."

Eva sat on the bed opposite Del's great-grandfather and patted the space next to her for friend to take the spot next to her. When Del raised her eyebrows, Eva said, "Can't you recognize when there's gonna be a story? Sit."

"Your friend is right," Robert said. "But only if you want to hear it."

Del swallowed and nodded. She had been waiting for answers so long. She took a seat next to Eva, and as she did, Robert Vesey solidified more. He wasn't yet like Jube, as solid-looking as a live person, but the shadows were lifting.

"Violet was such a happy child, always talking, laughing, and singing. She never seemed to have a down moment.

She loved learning magic and she was pretty good at it too. Rose and I were so proud of her. Ah, Rose." He shifted in the chair. "Now there is a woman who loves magic. She came to Nemmine Island as a young child, though people in her family had lived and attended school on the island for generations. It was such a delight for her to feel connected to the earth and her ancestors. Sharing that connection with students became her life's work. We did it together. Taught classes, maintained the grounds, improved our own spellwork, lived off the land, and did our best to raise our own family as we continued to build this community. But it was Rose who was always the heart of this place. Even though it was my ancestors that established the school, she was the one who came to embody it—Vesey Conservatory was like a second child to her. When Rose was too busy on a Saturday with her responsibilities as the head of the school, Violet used to joke and say, 'Mom's taking care of her other kid, let's go fishing.' The one day she decided to stay and help her mother, though, was the day I went out alone—and suffered a heart attack."

"Oh no." Both Del and Eva breathed the words at the same time.

"I don't know exactly what happened to them after that because I couldn't make it back to the island. Not even as a ghost, to bring either one of them any comfort." He sighed. "But I do know from having lost people myself when I was younger that people deal with loss in different ways. It can make some people cling together, but it can make others close themselves off from the people they should be holding tighter to." Robert Vesey sat up straighter in the chair. It was easier to see him now. He had a kind, young-looking face. "People don't always do the sensible thing in moments of loss or grief. Sometimes they want to look strong, and the only way they can think of is to hide their hurt. Be alone or work long hours or even travel long distances."

Del stroked her hand over Gramma's broom. *Hiding their hurt.* That was what Gramma had done whenever Del pressed for a story about her mother. And she kept her whole past locked up in a box rather than share it with Del and Dad. She just tried to go on as usual, and the pain had never gone away. Was that what Nana Rose had done to Gramma when her husband died?

Verses from "Not Another Day" filled Del's mind as she put together the information she had with Robert Vesey's words, and the meaning became clear. The song was not about some ex-boyfriend of Gramma's. It was about her father. And her mother.

There's an empty space
That used to be his place
Here within my heart

Heartache should have brought us close
Now when I need you the most
You have disappeared

There's a wall between us
Even in the hall I can't see us
Ever getting to okay

A wall. Could that be the wall Del was looking at now, separating Nana Rose's room from Gramma's? It was more than just a wall, though. Del guessed from what Gramma had written in her diary that Nana Rose never let Gramma see she was grieving. She just worked harder to try to forget.

And so, Gramma never learned how to discuss tough things. Neither one of them talked when they both needed to. And because of that, Gramma left. Even though she didn't really want to. She wrote it in the third verse:

I stand under this oak tree
And wonder why you can't see
That I'm barely holding on

And so I'm leaving
On that bus this evening
Why can't you ask me to stay?

270

It was all clicking into place in her mind. But if this was what the song was really about, then there must be some reason she mentioned an oak tree. . . .

"I have a question," Del asked. "One that you might be able to answer." She told him about the song and recited the lyric for him.

He smiled, and looked even more solid and real in that moment. "So she *did* make herself a hit record." He clapped his hands. "As far as oak trees go, we have a lot of them on the property."

Del tapped her finger along the broom. "I had thought of that lyric before, when I watergazed with Gramma. Is there one specific tree she might have been referring to?"

"No, but—"

"Ooh," Eva said, "maybe she carved something into a particular tree?"

"Girls—"

"Or she, I don't know, buried something under one?" Del offered.

"I know where the shovels are—" Eva began.

"You girls aren't gonna dig up the island's trees!" Robert Vesey laughed. "Besides, you haven't figured out the real meaning of that lyric. It's because you're still pretty new to conjuring. I'm give you a hint. Up."

Eva and Del stood up, resting the handles of the brooms on the floor, bristles up as they'd been taught.

"What are broom bristles made of?" he asked.

"Sorghum." Del and Eva chorused.

"Good. What are broom handles made out of?"

"They can be made of different types of wood, I think," Del said, looking at her gramma's broom.

"That's right. But once you graduate Vesey, you get a full-size *oaken* broom." He pointed. "Like that one."

Del looked at Gramma's broom. While it wasn't much heavier, it was certainly taller than her starter broom. Even taller than she was. And she was standing under it.

She imagined her gramma standing in this exact room, holding her broom in this exact way as she made her decision to leave Vesey and her mother behind. While her broom wasn't really an oak tree, Del had learned that was exactly what they symbolized in conjure magic. Tree roots connected with each other, they provided shade, safety, even nourishment.

Protect. Educate. Survive.

Knowing that motto, it must have been a hard choice for her gramma to make.

" . . . But Gramma never did any magic again," Del whispered.

"Maybe not like the magic here," Robert said. "But I saw those memories of yours flash by when you were in that pool. Your grandmother taught you how to make floorwash and clean a new house. That is part of Southern conjure. She even added rose petals to strengthen family

272

bonds." He closed the diary. His hands were clearly visible now, even though Del could see through them. "Violet remembers, and maybe without even realizing, has taught you some things that connect you to this island. I just wish she could find her own way to reconnect to it."

"There's only one person who can help her do that," Del said, putting the advertisement back in the diary and the diary in her pocket. She took a final look around her grandmother's room. "Nana Rose."

Eva nodded. "Let's get outta here."

The trio left the room through the portal and back out into the office, the door sealing closed behind them.

"Good afternoon, girls."

Del and Eva gasped, jumping almost a foot off the floor in surprise. They hadn't seen the older woman standing in the corner of the office. In one hand she held her own broom. In the other, she held Del's, her phone still tied to the bristles. Del glanced around her, but Robert Vesey's ghost was nowhere to be found.

"Now I see what your little ruse was about," she continued.

"Sorcell Rose—" Eva began.

"We weren't doing anything wrong, you know, we were trying to . . ." Del's words failed her. How was she going to get Nana Rose to listen to her now? Especially given the look on her great-grandmother's face?

"Hello, Rose." Robert Vesey's voice filled the office.

She looked around the room. "Bobby?"

The sun through the windows filtered through Robert Vesey's transparent form, making him shimmer, and harder to see. Del rushed over to close the blinds as Nana Rose placed Del's broom on her desk and sank heavily into her chair.

"I thought you'd left us," she said, finally.

"I couldn't get back before, darlin'. I couldn't get through the protection spell."

"I didn't . . ." Nana Rose put her head in her hand. "All this time, it was my fault you couldn't—"

"No, no. It was no one's fault." He kneeled at her feet. "I'm here now. Because your great-gran was determined to figure out why her family had split apart." Nana Rose tried to touch his face, but her hands went straight through. "I'm getting there," he said. "Soon."

She nodded and looked to Del.

"I didn't know anything about magic before I came here," Del said. "You told me this island was my legacy, built by my family, but I didn't feel that way. No one had told me this place existed—that *you* existed—and I felt just as lonely and out of place as I always have. I was desperate to know what happened between you and Gramma, to understand why things were this way, but neither one of you wanted to tell me about it. So I had to solve the mystery on my own. Well, with Eva's help."

Nana Rose sighed heavily, and her perfectly straight

shoulders slumped a little. She placed the handle of her own broom on the floor, leaning it against her desk. Her gaze ran over both girls finally stopping on the broom in Del's left hand. Her eyes grew misty as if she was trying to hold back tears.

"That was your grandmother's," she said.

"I guessed," Del replied, twirling the handle in her fingers. "I found it in the room."

"I'm surprised it allowed you to catch it."

"It didn't exactly *allow* me, but I figured it out. I thought Gramma might want it back."

Nana Rose took a deep breath. "I don't know if that's the case." She saw the diary shoved into the waistband of Del's shorts. "I found that diary, long ago. I'd lost Violet and I didn't know why. I knew it wasn't right to read it, but my sadness and need overcame me, and I tried to open it. It wouldn't give me permission, though."

"Do you know now?" Del asked, softly. "Why she left?"

Nana Rose nodded. "I . . . wasn't there for her when Bobby died. She loved him so much. I thought that since I now had to do the job of two people just keeping the school going, keeping us clothed and fed and sheltered was enough. And in the meantime, the school needed to continue. Our past needed to be presented, our people needed their education. I threw myself into the school, to keep it going, to keep the magic protected, to survive. . . ." Tears clouded her voice and she cleared her throat. "I'd lost the love of my life and I couldn't accept it. If I didn't keep going, keep working, I would fall apart. And I couldn't let Violet see me like that."

Del offered her the diary, which opened in Nana Rose's lap. "I think she needed to know the two of you could be sad together." Del put her hand on her great-grandmother's arm. "But it's not too late."

"I fear it might be, Del," she said. "This is not the sort of thing that can be mended through watergazing."

"I know," Del said, and she did. She also had a plan. The start of one, anyway. "Do you know of a spell named the Calling?"

Nana Rose put a hand over her mouth. "That's advanced magic. Where did you learn about that?"

"I read about it in a book in the library the other night, when everyone was asleep."

"How did you come to be in the library when—" Nana Rose began, and cut herself off. "Never mind. I don't want to know. The Calling is a spell that can connect people over very long distances in a much more profound way than watergazing. But it's a difficult conjure. And it can't be done alone."

"Well then it's a good thing you're not on your own," said Bobby Vesey, smiling his wide, white smile. "You have a great-granddaughter who's proving herself to be a promising witch. And I'll be there with you. I'm still getting the hang of this ghost thing, but I think I know of a penpun who'll show me the ropes."

Nana Rose nodded and Del snagged a few tissues from the box on the desk and placed them in her great-grandmother's hands.

"It was so hard after Bobby was gone. I didn't pay enough attention to Violet. I didn't help her with the grief the way I should have—"

Del hugged her. "It's okay, Nana Rose. You did the best you could at the time." After seeing her gramma fall and have to go to the hospital, Del understood how worry and pain and fear can cause you to make bad decisions. Ever since she got to Nemmine Island, she'd been making some pretty bad decisions herself. It was time to make a good one. "You . . . you were hurting too."

She dabbed her eyes and cheeks with the tissues, and said, "You don't have to say that, Del. I know the mistakes I made."

"I'm not just saying it. I know for sure because it's at the end of her most famous song."

In that moment, Del's broom flew to her side. Del beamed, and untied her phone from the handle. There might not be any internet connection here, but Del didn't need that to play "Not Another Day"—the song was saved in her library.

Ask me back to stay
Cause I can't take
Not another day living this way
Without you
Without you
Without you

As the final chorus faded away, Del stopped the playback.

"That's beautiful," Eva said in a quiet voice.

"I always thought that song was about some boy she'd loved," Del said. "But now I wonder if maybe she hoped you'd hear it and ask her to come home. I think she was scared to ask you."

"Well, now I have heard the song." Nana Rose took a deep breath and stood. "And I think it's time we head over to the Hall of Brooms."

"Come on, Eva," Del said, gently taking hold of her broom.

"Not this time." Eva shook her head.

"What do you mean?"

Eva tucked her broom under one arm and her sketchbook under the other. "I've helped you along up to here, but this sounds like a Vesey thing. A way to help your even bigger family get even stronger."

"But this is serious conjure," Del began. "I don't know what I'm doing. It's only with your help that I—"

Eva booped her nose. "You can do it. And I expect to hear the full story when it's all over. Every detail."

Del glanced over at Nana Rose and Papa Robert. Papa Robert . . . where had that name come from? Perhaps the same place as Nana Rose, Del guessed. It fit.

"The spell won't work without you," Papa Robert said.

She dragged in a deep breath. "Let's go to the hall."

23

This was the place where everything connected.

The Hall of Brooms was an enormous room on the third floor of the house, a place in the house Del hadn't been to before. Even though she'd seen it on the map her first day here, it hadn't been a place her teachers had taken her to, or a place she felt she needed to visit during her search for answers about Gramma. Now, though, standing in the awe-inspiring chamber, she wished she had.

While there was no dust or cobwebs, Del got the feeling no one had been up here in a long, long time. There was a calm silence that made her feel secure in the power of this place. It felt right, somehow, that her search had led her here.

The room had a wood floor, polished to such a fine gloss Del could see herself in it. She walked the perimeter of the room, mouth open in awe. This was a majestic place. Brooms of various shapes and sizes stood upright, their handles placed in stands that coiled into a spiral toward the center of the room. There were bristles of every color and length. None of the brooms living here had crisp, new bristles like hers—all were softened and frayed at the tips by use, some bent to the left or to the right. One even had separated in the middle, the sorghum turned outward to each side like an old-fashioned handlebar mustache.

Knowledge and strength radiated from the assembled brooms. Del could feel it all moving around her, sliding closer to where she stood. It nudged her like a curious kitten, and Del stood stock-still, too amazed to move until it returned to the spiral.

"The brooms of all Vesey sorcells who have gone before are housed here." Nana Rose's gentle voice held reverence. "Each time one of us passes on, their broom is installed here to preserve its wisdom and understanding in case it is ever needed."

"Whoa," Del breathed, turning in a circle. It looked like a forest of brooms and in her mind another connection from lore class fell into place. Brooms did symbolize trees.

And while a tree could grow alone, they thrived more when they were connected, their roots intertwining and feeding each other.

Nana Rose smiled. "Yes, I feel it too. We don't use this room often, but there is a certain power here that makes a person stand in awe."

"Can I touch them?"

"Yes, carefully."

Del walked the line of multicolored brooms. A light ringing sounded in her ears as she touched them with her fingertips. It wasn't harsh or loud; it was as though someone whispered a secret, then drifted away. Light from the descending sun filtered into the room, lending the off- white walls softer hues of pink and ripe peach. Each broom's shadow fell across the floor making a spiral pattern on the floorboards.

"That's . . . my broom," Papa Robert said.

Nana Rose held her hand out to him. This time she was able to grasp it and they crossed the floor together, stopping at the open end of the spiral. Papa Robert stood next to his broom. It had a faded purple handle and pale, frayed bristles bound together with light blue cord. Fishing lures were braided into the broom straw, along with a few small metal circles on a length of wire that bound the straw to the handle.

"Since his broom is the last one on the spiral, does

that mean you were the last Vesey sorcell who died?" Del asked.

"I suppose it does," he answered, looking at his wife.

Nana Rose nodded, as if she didn't trust herself to speak. Then she cleared her throat. "Yes. We've been . . . very lucky to have not lost more people in forty years."

A wave of loss rolled over Del. She swallowed it down but it sat like a stone in her belly. If Gramma had taught her mother the magic, would her broom be installed here in this spiral that bound them all together?

Del walked along the wall, her broom in one hand and her gramma's in the other. She felt full, like someone had just poured her to overflowing. The light must have been brighter here because her vision seemed sharper than usual. Around her the air tasted cleaner as she breathed in through her mouth. Her ears still rang, but now it sounded more like she was in a room full of people having different conversations. It felt like a celebration was going on. A party.

And they just needed one more guest.

"Are you ready to do this?" Del asked.

"I don't know, child. It's been so long since . . ." Nana Rose turned away from Del, moved to the opening of the spiral. She pressed her lips together.

Del came to her side then. After she tucked both brooms under one arm, she pressed her free hand against

Nana Rose's arm. "No more holding in secrets, remember? You promised."

Nana Rose kept her eyes on the spiral as she nodded. She swallowed hard, then looked over at her great-granddaughter. "I am scared, Delphinia. Scared too much time has passed. Scared she won't want to talk about what happened. That she won't want to hear how—" Her voice cracked as she twisted her hands together. "I have made so many mistakes. Held my feelings in too deep. And I was too proud to admit it. Even when she contacted me about you coming here."

Del recognized what Nana Rose was going through because she had done the same thing all her life. Held on to her feelings about moving every year, about not having any close friends or deep family roots. Pretending it was okay when Gramma avoided her requests for information about her mom. Her deepest wish was something she never even knew she wanted: close ties to a community, the chance to be a part of something bigger than herself, her dad, and her gramma. It was only because of her time here at Vesey that she understood what she was allowed to want, and what waited for her when she accepted the truth of it.

Del said, "Everyone makes mistakes. You're lucky—you have a chance to fix yours and spend time with your daughter. Gramma can't do that."

Eyes shimmering with tears, Nana Rose took in a deep

284

breath and let it out slowly. She cradled her broom close. This time, when she looked at Del, her head was held high. "You know, for a troublesome great-gran, you're a pretty smart child."

"I can be sometimes." Del grinned. "Besides, I know that Gramma's wanted to talk to you for a long, long time." Del shifted the brooms from under her arm to laying them on her shoulder. "I always knew her song was about losing someone she loved. It was about losing you, losing her dad, and losing her connection to this place, to conjure."

After a little nod, Nana Rose said, "Well, we shouldn't make her wait *not another day*."

Del held up both brooms. "Let's do it!"

Nana Rose led the way, describing the spell as she did. While she and Papa Robert would set their brooms to anchor the spell, it would be Del who completed the ritual, who would call out to Gramma. Del was Gramma's descendant, and that held a special place in Southern conjure. If the newest generation called out to their elders for help, those elders could not help but respond. Nana Rose took her place at the end of the spiral. She set the handle of her broom down in the stand next to her husband's. The moment she did so, the air in the room shifted. Papa Robert grasped his broom. He wore a suit now, with a colorful tie and an expression of pride that made Del's chest swell with her own sense of purpose. Del used her broom to wave at him.

This was the right thing to do and the right time to do it. She'd found a community to belong to and family that welcomed her. All she had to face now was one more fear: that the magic wasn't hers and she couldn't do it correctly.

Del pushed all the negative thoughts out of her head. She kept them out by repeating the same phrase over and over in her mind: *You are connected. You are a part of conjure. Conjure is a part of you.* Then she placed her gramma's broom in the next stand beside Nana Rose's, pressing it carefully until it locked into place. A rush of air passed, as though Del was standing on the sidewalk and a huge truck whizzed by. It was so fast and strong, it almost took her breath away. She gasped, her knees going weak.

She looked over at Nana Rose, who still stood by her broom. The watergazing spell, the chewing gum spell she'd done with Eva—these were nothing compared to this. Del could feel the energy from the assembled brooms swirling around the entire room. It lifted her braids, battering them against her face and neck. She squeezed her eyes closed. She wanted to call out to Nana Rose that she needed help, but the wind-like energy took her voice away. She fought to stay upright in the gale. With her free hand, she shoved her braids out of her face and looked down at the floor. How was she supposed to place her broom to complete the spell if she couldn't even see the stand?

Frustrated, Del looked up toward the ceiling and gasped. A swirling spiral of clouds had gathered above her.

Within them, Del could see vague shapes moving. They were dark, indistinct figures, similar to how her great-grandfather had looked when she first saw him. And she knew in that moment why the spell was named the Calling. Because these were her people, some who hadn't lived in a long time, here to help her accomplish this task.

All the previous owners of the brooms installed in the Hall of Brooms were here, swirling and roiling, waiting for Del to state her wish, to place her broom and complete the spiral. Like she learned in Sorcell Harus's classroom that first day: the broom didn't change energy. The broom gave it a path to travel in order to help the conjurer in times of need. Placing her broom in the stand would do the same thing as touching the handle to the earth. But instead of using the earth's power, Del would be using the combined power of her people: witches who came before her and devoted their time and love and spirit to preserving Southern conjure.

Pushing against the wind, Del stood up straight and tall. She still couldn't see the stand on the floor, but she could see Nana Rose and Papa Robert. They each stood beside their brooms, watching her. Because she could use them as a marker, Del could estimate where she'd put Gramma's broom. She leaned forward, pushing her shoulder against the increasing wind and headed toward where Gramma's broom should be. The sound of the chimes and shells on the brooms were drowned out by the roar of the wind. But she made it by putting one foot in front of the other. Soon, she touched Nana Rose's arm.

"Smart girl."

Del thought it was Nana Rose's voice saying those words over the winds but she couldn't be sure. She turned and headed back toward the end of the spiral again, her free hand out in front of her. Gramma's broom should be . . . right . . . about . . .

There it was! She closed her fingers over the bristles of Gramma's broom. Now to find her own place in the spiral. Two, three, four more steps in the bracing winds felt like an eternity, but now she was here. But there was too much wind and swirling to see the floor clearly. She tapped the handle of her broom on the floor searching for the stand.

That was when her broom gently shifted in her hands. It was guiding her.

The click of the broom's handle locking onto its place on the spiral was loud. Quickly, she voiced her wish knowing it would be heard even over the storm.

"We need my gramma. We need to see her, talk to her."

Instantly, the howling of winds stopped. The clouds above her circled over and over, and then the spirits within dropped, one by one, to solidify next to their brooms. A range of faces in shades of brown appeared around the spiral. They were dressed in all manner of clothing: some in long, flowing dresses and spiffy suits, others wrapped snugly in brightly colored cloth printed with various patterns. Some with long braids like Del's, others with heads bald like the triplets, and everything in between.

From the middle of the spiral, a dot of orange light appeared. It pulsed, then grew, widening until it filled the entire center. From there the light radiated outward, curving along the spiral, stopping at each of Del's ancestors for brief moment before moving on to the next. As the light grew closer to Del, she could feel a gentle warmth ebbing from it. There was a hush now in the Hall of Brooms, like every soul and spirit inside this room was waiting for what was about to happen.

Del had no idea what the spell would do. Would Gramma's face appear in the light? Could they talk with her as if she was there in person? The light crept closer, growing brighter as it passed each broom and its conjurer. As Del watched, she realized what the light was doing as it moved toward her and Nana Rose. A path emerged from the spiral. No, not a pathway, Del realized. A portal. But from where?

The light stopped at Papa Robert, illuminating the floor at his feet. Nana Rose and Del turned to face the lit path, Nana Rose wringing her hands and Del holding her breath. Already she could tell this was a strong connection—much stronger than the one she'd accomplished with her watergazing. For this communication required help and support. She gazed at her ancestors and their brooms, all standing along different parts of the spiral and knew this was where she belonged. All the people who had learned and taught Southern conjure here showed up because Del had asked them to. These were the people who had fought to keep the magic she was learning alive. She had connections with her people through time, without ever having known them. Because of these people, she could be the person she was growing up to be. Her heart swelled with pride. She was part of something way bigger than herself. Something way older too. Someday she would be among these people, these spirits.

But someone was missing. Until . . .

"No way," Del whispered. "It can't be."

But it was.

Footsteps echoed from within the portal, growing closer with each breath Del took. A shadow lengthened along the path, until finally Del saw her.

"Gramma!"

Del screeched with joy, then covered her mouth with her hands. She started to run to her and hug her as tight as she could. But Nana Rose stopped her.

"Let her exit the calling spiral, Del. Don't run in there. No telling where that portal might take you."

Bouncing up and down on the balls of her feet, Del impatiently waited for her gramma to step off the lit pathway leading away from the spiral portal. Once she did, the light slowly faded away, leaving her grandmother standing in front of Del, leaning heavily on a cane with a small bag over her shoulder, looking like her old self, not like the person who Del had last seen in the hospital bed.

Finally, she could run up to her gramma. "You're here!"

"I am, baby," Gramma said, opening her arms. "Because of you. I'm so proud of you."

Del fell into her embrace. "Careful," Gramma said. "Hug me on my left side."

"Oh, sorry." Del shifted and hugged her again. "I didn't do it alone, Gramma. Everyone here gave a little of their own power to the spell so it could be as strong as possible. I was the final part."

Del's grandmother looked around the room at all the spirits and their brooms standing in the hall. There were tears in her eyes when she said, "You were a very important part."

Then Del took her gramma's hand and led her over to where Nana Rose and Papa Robert stood.

"Hi, Pop. I missed you," Gramma said.

"I missed you too, my girl." His voice rumbled, and he embraced her.

Gramma leaned against his shoulder before turning to Nana Rose. Del held her breath as the two most important women in her life regarded each other. It felt like a lifetime passed, and still, neither one of them said anything.

So Del did.

"Gramma, I know how lonely you felt after Papa Robert died. Nana Rose was lonely too, but she didn't tell you." Del grasped her grandmother's arm. "I understand. The way you felt, it's the same way I feel when I think about Mom."

Her gramma's eyes widened and she stammered a reply. "I didn't think you felt— I mean, I didn't realize—"

"I know, I know," Del reassured her. "That's why I'm telling you. In our family, we don't talk to each other when we feel lonely or hurt and we don't admit when we need help. I'm guilty of it too. But two new friends I've met here—Eva and my broom—are helping me learn to ask for help when I need it. It's a lot less lonely."

Nana Rose and Gramma exchanged looks with each other. "Maybe we both can learn alongside you," Nana Rose said.

"That would be good. I miss my mom a lot, and I don't even have any memories of her." Del tucked a loose braid behind her ear, looking at Gramma. "I'm hoping you'll finally share yours with me."

Gramma smiled and nodded. "I'm gonna do my best, baby."

"Thank you," Del said. Then she put a hand on her hip and looked back and forth between Gramma and Nana Rose.

Nana Rose took a deep breath and spoke first. "Oh,

Violet. I should have been there for you when your father died. But I couldn't see through my own pain enough to help you with yours and for that, I will always be so, so sorry."

"I felt like I'd lost both of you, even though you were still alive." Gramma leaned on her cane, a tear running down her cheek. "To me, leaving was my only option. Once I was gone, I wanted to come back. I was too ashamed to admit that."

"You could have always come back, dear heart. I've been right here waiting, hoping every day that you would." Nana Rose clutched the crumpled tissues in one hand.

"So, are you two gonna hug it out or what? I've got studying to do, you know."

Laughter erupted from all those gathered in the hall. With smiles still on their faces, Gramma and Nana Rose embraced each other in a tight hug. They rocked side to side while hugging, as if they were trying to keep their balance.

"Oh, my baby is home!" Nana Rose's voice was so full of joy that it brought tears to Del's eyes.

After they parted, everyone in the room came together to thank the ancestors and wish them well on their journeys. Finally, Del had brought Nana Rose and Gramma back together. She hadn't done it alone—she had the help of so many others who had lived here before her. People who had committed to sharing their knowledge with the community of conjurers here on Nemmine Island. She had managed to unite many generations of magic users to come to assist her. And for once, knowing that she needed help felt right.

24

It was here all too soon: the final day of the summer session at Vesey Conservatory for the Wonder Arts. And it was time to go home.

For the first time in her life, Del wasn't excited about leaving school. She wasn't ready to leave everything she'd learned and everyone she'd met. The last two weeks with Gramma on Nemmine Island had been incredible. At first, Del worried that Gramma and Nana Rose not having seen each other for almost forty years would make their reunion awkward and difficult. But she should have known that both her favorite conjurers wouldn't let a silly thing like time apart make them uncomfortable with each other.

After they spoke more in the Hall of Brooms, there were lots of hugs and tears before all three of them went into Nana Rose's office. There, Gramma brought out the memory case from her bag and shared the magazine and newspaper articles about her first record, the one you could still hear on the radio and find on YouTube. She told a story about Del's mom, Daisy, who at Del's age had set up a lemonade and advice stand in their neighborhood. She'd made way more money on the advice than the lemonade! There were photos and greeting cards and ticket stubs, each one with its own lively tale.

"Thank you, Gramma." Del hugged her and kissed her cheek.

"You're welcome, baby. I'm just sorry I didn't do it sooner."

"Better late than never." Full of stories to hold close, she left the two women in Nana Rose's office and shut the door. Del knew they had lots to talk about. While she only listened at the door for a few minutes, Del had the feeling her grandmother and great-grandmother talked long into the night.

In the morning, Del proudly introduced Gramma to everyone and finally told her classmates that Nana Rose was her great-grandmother. It felt good to admit the secret she'd been keeping since she arrived on the island. As important as it had seemed at the time, it felt a bit silly now, her pretending to be something she wasn't. She was accepted for who she was and for what she wanted to be—not because she was a conjurer, but because she was part of the community. She knew that now. And so did Gramma.

Because they both wanted to repair their relationship and not waste any more time apart, Del didn't have a hard time convincing her gramma and her great-grandmother to teach classes together. Well, Nana Rose taught and Gramma shared her memories of being a student at Vesey herself. The students loved hearing about Gramma's escapades learning conjure. She shared what came easily to her and what was so hard she had to practice over and over until she was exhausted. And somehow, after so long, she still remembered a lot of the spells.

The South really is a portal. Or at least this island was. Since coming through the spiral, it was like Gramma had come back in time as she came to the island. She looked exactly the same, but her aches and pains began to heal and she had more energy to do spells and share the contents of her memory case with both of them. She was more like the Gramma Del remembered from years ago. Most exciting was introducing her to Eva, who had already heard so much about her.

And now, it was all over. Del stood on the front porch of the great house with all the sorcells, including her gramma, as the parents and guardians of the students came to pick them up. Yes, it was still hot. Yes, the sun was still bright enough to sting her eyes. But Del didn't care anymore. She'd had the best experience she'd ever had at any school she'd ever been in and she didn't want to let it go so soon. She sucked in a deep breath of steamy air, then let it out.

When Del felt someone watching her this time, she glanced around, unafraid. She had her broom with her, she had her friends, and she had her family. She was protected, educating herself on conjure magic, and she would do what she could to make sure the magic survived in her. She turned to find Ol' Lundy watching the proceedings from a sheltered, grassy spot near the water's edge. When he saw that Del was looking at him, he thumped his tail on the ground and opened his mouth wide in what she hoped was a gator smile. Del could feel the gentle vibration of magic that flowed through this island, the people who lived here, and now herself.

Del wanted to leave her mark on this island. She wanted people to remember she'd been here. She wanted to be a part of this island's history and part of the magic that had lived here for centuries. She held her broom in a loose grip, but it moved anyway, leaning itself against her shoulder. Eva had given her a shell she'd collected from the beach when she'd arrived and Del had promised to add it to her broom. It would be the first thing she did when she got back to Delaware.

Kids shouted and tumbled around outside, soaking up the last of the sun and fun on the green lawn that never seemed to need cutting. They exchanged email address and phone numbers, and shared promises to see each other when the regular school year started. Del sat on the porch of the house and watched family members come to pick up their kids to take them home. The triplets' grandparents came to get them first—an elderly couple wearing matching T-shirts that had "Dennis Family Reunion" printed on the front. All three girls wished Del pleasant dreams before they headed off to the pier to board their family boat. Then both of Fino's dads arrived and they brought a gift basket for Nana Rose. Joyce's older sister arrived next. She tossed her little sis a motorcycle helmet that Joyce tucked under her arm while saying her goodbyes to everyone. They both waved as they headed in the opposite direction of the pier, down the path toward the beach to climb aboard the boat steered by one of Lundy's young'uns.

Del and Eva sat side by side, each with their brooms nearby, watching all the other students depart. They waved goodbye until their arms hurt.

"This was an amazing summer!" Eva said, leaning back on her elbows.

"And there's still so much time until school starts again," Del said.

Eva tapped her sandaled foot on the step. "You're right. That means there might be some more amazing stuff to come! That reminds me," Eva said, sitting up. "Let me give you my info."

Del took out her phone and handed it to Eva, who input her street address as well her email address and phone number. While Del would have loved to visit Eva, she didn't know when she would be able to return this way again. But if Gramma and Nana Rose could heal their decades-old hurts, maybe anything was possible. Del took the notebook and pen Eva held out to her and wrote her own information down in her best handwriting.

The moment Eva replaced the notebook with Del's information into her bag, a couple came up the path from the beach toward the big house, walking hand in hand. The woman was short and round-cheeked with tightly coiled black hair. The man was tall and thin, and had the reddest hair and beard Del had ever seen. When Eva saw them, she leaped up from her place on the porch beside Del and ran to them.

"Mom, Dad!" They scooped her up and swung her around while Eva chatted nonstop to them so fast Del couldn't even keep up with her words. Before Del knew it, she'd dragged them over to the porch.

"This is Del," Eva said proudly.

They spoke until the sun began to slowly lower in the sky and Eva's mom said it was time to get home. They headed toward the shoreline while Eva said a special good-bye to Del.

"Will you come back for the full school year?"

"I don't know if I can." Del pressed her lips together tightly.

She could tell Eva was disappointed. But when she spoke, Eva said, "It's okay. When you do know, you can find the closest bowl of water and call me."

"Can I hug you goodbye?" Del asked.

Instead of answering, Eva launched herself at Del, hugging her tight enough to make her eyes water. Del didn't care. "Of course, duh! Remember, we did the friendship spell. We'll stick together no matter what."

Del just hugged her friend tighter.

Finally, Eva released her and raced after her parents. Del watched the trio until they disappeared around the path to the beach and the waiting boats. She knew she'd be able to call up the memory of these weeks to keep her warm, even when the colder northern winters set in. The gators, the marsh, even the wild pigs were stories she'd be able to tell forever. Her friendship with Eva and discovering the mystery of why her ties with Nemmine Island had been cut so long ago were the biggest successes she had. That and her broom. It was becoming her companion and even starting to forgive her for her earlier disbelief in magic.

"There's no way I'm leaving you behind," she said to the broom. It didn't respond, but Del sensed it was pleased with her decision.

The island seemed softer now that all the other kids had left. Quieter. Breeze flew in from the ocean, salty and cool, pushing out the heat of the day for a few precious moments. Now that no kids shouted and played, the sounds of the marsh and garden life prevailed. Leaves and grain rustled in the floral-scented air. Marsh bubbles popped as fish leaped and splashed in the water. Del saw a mosquito try to land on her leg and she shooed it away.

"I'm the last to get here and the last to leave," she said.

"You were a joy to teach, Del." It was Sorcell Nyla, who smiled as she adjusted her headwrap.

Sorcell Harus nodded. "I appreciated your enthusiasm for conjure. You did well."

Del smiled and leaned back against one of the columns supporting the porch. "You both taught me a lot. Thank you."

Nana Rose tapped her broom handle gently on the porch, then stood from the rocking chair she was in. "Del, walk with me, please." She traipsed down the steps to the lawn.

Del glanced over her shoulder and both sorcells nodded while Gramma shooed her off.

She caught up to Nana Rose and they walked, slowly, across the bright green lawn to the edge of the tree line, where the live oak spread its branches low and wide to give seats among its papery leaves. Nana Rose chose a branch and leaned against it, her broom nestled in the crook of her arm. Del chose a branch too, one that curved closer to the ground, and pushed herself up with one hand to sit comfortably in the tree's hold.

"What did you want to talk about?" Del asked.

She laughed gently. "After so many years without family here, I could talk for a whole month and not be finished." She looked up into the live oak's branches. "But we don't have time. So I'll just say this—"

Nana Rose paused and Del held her breath, waiting and wondering.

"Thank you for everything you've done for me. You had no knowledge of conjure when you came here, and it would have been easy for you to dismiss it, to be afraid of it, or refuse to believe in it. But you didn't do any of those things. And that's renewed my hope that conjure will survive. In our family and out there in the world."

"I'm going to do my best," Del said. She swung her legs, bouncing on the tree branch, the broom tucked firmly under her arm. She gazed at the sky. A trio of birds circled, then as a fourth and fifth joined them, they arrowed up into bright blue sky and out of sight. Together.

Too soon, Nana Rose said, "We should head back."

Del launched herself off the branch while Nana Rose used her broom to balance as she stood. They walked back in a comfortable silence that spoke of happiness and contentment. Someone was on the porch with Gramma and the sorcells when Del and Nana Rose got closer. Even though the person was shadowed in the dimmer light under cover of the porch, Del recognized that shadow immediately. She shouted and started running.

"Dad!"

"Hey, sweetheart!" He jogged down the porch stairs and headed toward Del. His face was all smiles as he swept her up in a huge hug and spun her around. He was in his service uniform, Air Force blue trousers and light blue short-sleeved shirt. The plastic name tag on his chest pressed into her arm, but she didn't mind. It was so good to see him.

"I didn't know you were coming. I thought Nana Rose was going to take us back in her boat."

He set her down on her feet and straightened up to his full height before speaking. "Well, I thought I'd surprise you."

Del glanced up at Gramma. "Did you know about this?"

Gramma's grin was mischievous. "Oh, maybe I did. One thing no one can accuse me of is not being able to keep a secret."

"Just promise me that these will be the only kinds of secrets we keep anymore."

Del's dad looked from Del to Gramma to Nana Rose and back again. "I get the sense something major happened here. Is someone going to fill me in?"

"I will," Del said. "When we're on the road."

Dad nodded, his eyebrows raised. "Looking forward to hearing that story."

"Well, I guess we should be heading out," Gramma said, getting up from the rocking chair she'd been sitting in.

"Maybe one day, Del, you'll be back?" Nana Rose asked, hopefully.

"I really wish I could come back for the regular school year. I'd like to learn more about conjure and its history. But maybe we can visit soon." Del looked hopefully at her great-grandmother and wondered how she ever could have thought she wasn't part of her family.

"I would love that." A full, real smile from Nana Rose brightened her day even more than Eva's flashing braces.

Del's dad placed one hand on his chin as if he was considering something. "If secrets are an issue, and it seems as though they are, I should probably reveal the one I have now, rather than keep it for later."

"You have a secret?" Del's heart pounded. She wasn't sure she could handle another family mystery. At least not this soon. "What is it?" she asked, wearily.

"Remember before you came here, I told you I only had a short time left before I could retire?" Del nodded and held her breath. "Well, I've got my assignment for those two years." His face was serious as he pulled out a

305

piece of paper from his pocket. "This says my new duty assignment is at Charleston Air Force Base. Just a short drive away."

Del opened her mouth, but didn't know what to say.

"We might not be able to get here by September," Dad went on, "but maybe in January you can enroll here, if you want to." He looked over at Nana Rose. "If you think there might be any openings available."

"There will always be a place here for Del." Nana Rose turned to her daughter. "And for you, Violet."

"Rose and Violet," Del mused. "I saw that one of the boats is called *The Flower Girls*. Does that mean the two of you?"

"It means all of us," Gramma said.

"But my name isn't a flower," Del said. "Delphinia means dolphin. I looked it up once."

"Ah, but your name *does* come from a flower," Gramma said. "It's the plural of Delphinium, a flower shaped like a dolphin jumping out of the water."

"Really? Why didn't I know that?"

Gramma chuckled. "Because you never asked, I suppose."

Del threw up her hands and laughed too. "Well, there's a lot of things I want to learn about now."

"And I promise to teach you," Gramma said, putting her arm around Del. "*Protect, educate, survive.* I never forgot that." She reached out her other hand to Del's dad, and he climbed the stairs and took it. "I didn't educate Del before, but now that we're all together, we'll have the Vesey Conservatory for the Wonder Arts back on top in no time."

"As long as I've got you back in my life, we can handle anything together." Nana Rose smiled, leaning on her broom.

"I know that's right." Gramma gave Del a high five. "I might need a bit more practice before I'm ready to teach any more than basic conjure, though. I'm sure there's a lot I've forgotten."

For the first time in ever, Del wasn't upset about moving again. This time, she would have Nana Rose and the sorcells and even Eva anticipating her arrival. This time, she was looking forward to a new beginning in a new place, learning an old, important magic that continued to grow and make itself new again. Del tucked her broom tighter under arm, then gave her gramma a squeeze.

"That's okay, Gramma," she said, grinning up at her. "Everyone has to start somewhere. Even witches."

Acknowledgments

Heartfelt thanks to my mom for being an amazing listener and telling me that sometimes it's best to listen to myself. To my husband for being you. To my cousins, who are not from South Carolina but came down from up north every summer to visit. I hope you have cherished memories of those times.

To Sara Makeba Daise for her support and her wonderful article, "Be Here Now: The South Is a Portal" published in *Root Work Journal*. I'm glad the portal opened to connect us.

There are others—too many to name here. I'll end with thanking everyone who has read, loved, shared, and recommended my work. I appreciate you.